Alice in Madland

Margaret Pitz

riverrun

For Hiag, with love and thanks

Also for Fran, Gillie, Nick, 'Westfield Security Officers'
and especially for 'Pearl'

ONE

27th January 1958

Dear Miss Chorley,

Thank you for attending the interview yesterday for the position of Library Clerk II.

We regret to inform you that your application has not been successful, inasmuch as we have selected another candidate.

Yours truly,

(signed) squiggle mcmdle

for Westfield Council Library

Bugger. I thought this one could have been the answer, and I might have quite enjoyed it, too, and now it's back to square minus-one.

But it wasn't; in the same post was a letter from the chief officer of another Westfield Council office, thanking me for my recent application for the position of Junior Clerk, and asking me to telephone him at my earliest convenience.

'Why do you think he wants me to phone?' I asked my mum.

'Perhaps he's in a hurry – and maybe it's so he can see how you are on the phone, I suppose.'

'How should I be?'

'You know how to be, Alice. Like the daughter of a retired army officer. Polite, business-like, deferential, warm and friendly. The sort of person he wants in his office, answering his phone for him. Just don't be cheeky and over-familiar.'

I did my best and got an interview for the very next day, at which I was told to start on the following Monday. It turned out that the girl who'd secured 'my' job at the library had already accepted this post at the security department, so they'd stopped looking. Evidently stacking shelves and dealing with book-borrowing people had more appeal (as well as more money) for her than typing envelopes and channelling phones calls for minor civil servants who were steeped in a sense of their own importance as they dealt with security issues for Westfield and its surrounds.

How different my life might have been for the next three years if she hadn't taken the library job and left me to the experience of Miss Brenda Pearl Taylor.

Being second choice - twice, if you count the library position - didn't trouble me at all. I was so very grateful to have the job, rather than humbling myself (as I saw it) by applying to the local laundry or box factory: the only options the local employment office had been able to come up with. I thought of myself as the daughter of an army officer and worthy of a 'nice' job, but evidently the Youth Employment Officer saw me as 'cheeky and over-familiar' and a failure at seventeen.

And so, really, did I. For as long as I could remember I had wanted to be a nursery nurse, a nanny. I was downright scathing about people who worked in shops or offices, became teachers, or went into regular nursing. I wanted to hold and love babies and play with small children. (I'd have liked my own, but often doubted anyone would find me attractive enough to even ask me out on a date, never mind ask me to marry him and bear his children.) I drifted through school, usually in a fantasy world of my own creation, assuring fellow students that Latin, French, History, Maths, Art, Gym, Lacrosse – you name it – were useless to me, because I was going to be a nanny. In my final miserable year (17% for Maths mock GCE) I applied to the prestigious Norland College for nanny training which we could never have afforded (and not a hope anyway with my nowhere-near-good-enough school record), St Christopher's Nursery Nurse

Training College (possibly just about affordable, but academically the same problem) and an orphanage in Swansea that was apparently under the aegis of the Church. Somewhat to my surprise but greatly to my relief, they offered me a place. Even better, not only did I not have to pay anything; they would actually pay me. It must have been the reference given to me by my oh-so-glad-to-be-rid-of-me headmistress: *Alice comes from a good family, her father being a retired army officer. She is cheerful, willing and honest.* Cheerful – oh yes, almost always; willing – well, sometimes; but honest? Not so much.

It would be wrong to blame the orphanage entirely for the disaster that followed. I might have been able to stick it out if I hadn't suddenly become the girlfriend of choice (coming in second, again) for one Jack Watson after months of watching him court Wendy Freeman – a girl who'd broken all records for achievement at school and had been offered a place at no less than five top universities. I couldn't imagine what they found to talk about, but on the other hand, I had no idea what we might talk about either. After she dumped him we, Jack and I, had no more than four dates before I left for Swansea, all of which took place at my home and consisted solely of heavy petting on the sofa directly below my parents' bedroom. I don't think we talked much about anything, but I was smitten and found it hard to leave him to start my new life at the Swansea Church Orphanage. He was my first real boyfriend and even though I knew he was heavily rebounding from Wendy, I was in heaven and convinced I was in love.

I think I was willing to make a go of it at the orphanage when I got there, despite not being met at Swansea Station as promised. But, ever resourceful, I got a taxi (my hope-for-the-best-but-be-prepared-for-the-worst mother had supplied me with quite a wad of cash 'just in case') and I was deposited at the edge of a long and dark drive down which I carried my much too heavy suitcase to announce my arrival at their front door.

It was pandemonium. Nobody knew who I was, although two girls swore they'd been at the station to meet me and that I'd ignored them. (I might have. I hadn't understood their heavily Welsh-accented question so I'd moved away from them, shaking my head and looking for I don't know what.) Nobody seemed to be in charge; Matron was apparently ill in bed with flu and three other girls were squabbling over how to make her some scrambled eggs. I hovered at the edge of the dark maroon-painted kitchen, shifting my suitcase out of the way of one and into the way of another, countless times. I don't remember wanting or eating any supper and I don't remember going to bed in the dormitory with eight skinny hard beds and a broken window letting in rain and cold, but I have a vague recollection of being woken next morning by the senior girl with a sense of amazement that I had actually slept, followed by a sense of crashing doom.

I seemed to be the only new girl, so I followed the others to the kitchen and copied them as they sliced stale bread and made themselves toast. One of them asked me if I wanted porridge, and when I said 'oh yes please,' she pointed out the dusty jar on a shelf over the cooker with what might have been porridge oats inside it. Somebody told me I was going to work in Room Three and somebody else told me that the children were being kept in bed as they all had colds. Room Three was another dark, tiny-windowed room at the top of the house and contained about twenty children about two and a half feet tall. The orphanage children were apparently sorted according to size so that all the clothes in each room fit all the children in it. I would guess they ranged in age from two to four and were about evenly divided into boys on one side of the room, girls on the other. They didn't look as if they wanted to play with me and I didn't really feel like hugging any of them with their snot-encrusted faces and vomit-streaked pyjamas.

It didn't matter. I obviously wasn't there to play anyway – I was there to sweep the floor, change all the wet and soiled beds, clean up the sick, take the stinking linen and clothes down to the laundry and bring up whatever was clean and dry-ish that belonged to Room Three. Each item had a large number three inked clearly and visibly on it, even their pyjamas. What this meant, of course, was that as soon as a Room Three child grew too big for these clothes, it was moved on to a larger child room, leaving behind any tentative relationships the poor soul had managed to forge. Feeling a despairing loneliness myself for my burgeoning connection with Jack, I found this hard to think about without wanting to cry.

On the way down I met Rita, whose job it was to scrub the stone stairs from top to bottom every day. She'd given up a job in Woolworths, she told me, to come here to train as a nursery nurse, and was thrilled with it all. 'I'm going to make these steps *sparkle,*' she informed me cheerily. In the laundry I met Pam who was hand-washing nappies and who'd been out of work for three years. She seemed slightly less grateful for the opportunity, but my pride in being accepted for a place at this 'training orphanage' nose-dived. Evidently getting a place there was like asking a bank if they'd keep your money for you.

The senior worker sort of took me under her wing, making sure I kept busy and telling me that because I was new I would have only one day off a week but would have two hours rest in the afternoon – during which I was expected to do some mending. When she thought I was used to working from 8am to 8pm I would get two days off a week. Everybody was expected to do mending in the evenings and probably on their days off, too.

I didn't last long enough to have a day off. I desperately missed Jack and absolutely hated the long dreary days of cleaning, mending, washing and washing up. After that first morning in room three I was assigned to kitchen chores and never saw the children again. In truth I didn't really want to – collectively they broke my heart, the more so because I knew I couldn't bring myself to hug and love them as I had always imagined. I told myself I'd be better with the babies, but it was probably just as well that I never set eyes on them, so haven't had to remember how heart-breaking they might have been.

On my fourth day I got a letter from Jack with S.W.A.L.K. written on the flap on the back of the envelope, and scrawled messages of 'missing you lots' inside. On a tidal wave of homesickness and yearning for him, I came to my decision. After lunch, instead of taking items from the never-ending pile of torn clothes in the ever-overflowing mending basket, I put on my coat, walked down to the station where I enquired about trains to my home town, and bought a single ticket for the next day, blessing my mother's foresight in providing me with enough necessary cash. I walked back up the steep hill to the orphanage and told a completely unmoved Pam and Rita that I was leaving. I didn't tell the senior worker, but having seen meal trays being taken into what I deduced was Matron's room, I knocked on her door, entered at her hoarsely barked command, and told her I couldn't go on and was leaving. I don't remember exactly what she said but it's not my impression that she was very nice about it, stating quite categorically that I should be ashamed to be so weak, and as far as she was concerned I was despicable and they had no further use for me. I didn't care; she wasn't saying anything that hadn't been said to me before, so I stood there and took it, knowing that absolutely nothing she could have said would have changed my mind. Eventually she succumbed to a paroxysm of coughing, so I said politely, 'Thank you, Matron' and backed out of the room, almost but not quite, bowing as I went. Next day I lugged my case down to the station and got on the first available train back to the Midlands.

I wasn't very well received at home. My mother was sorrowfully 'disappointed' in me (again) and my father didn't speak to me for six months.

'What the hell are *you* doing here?' was his opening sally, brusquely cutting short my stammering 'I couldn't bear it...' with 'Well, I have nothing more to say to you. Stay out of my sight.'

But I didn't care. For one thing I was ill with bronchitis (undoubtedly caught from the children in Room Three and not helped by sleeping in a rain-spattered bed) and for another, I would be seeing Jack again. I gave myself two weeks to get over it all and then started the demoralising process of finding a job that wouldn't offend my snobbish sensibilities. Hence the library non-starter, leading to the Council Security Office, their senior secretary, Miss Brenda Pearl Taylor and, ultimately, The Game.

TWO

It wasn't hard work. It was my job to type envelopes for any letters CSO Stevens had dictated to Pearl during the day (maybe five a week, more like two or three), make us all a coffee in the morning and some tea in the afternoon, and answer the tiny telephone switchboard, putting the occasional call through to the appropriate security officer. I rather enjoyed that, and I especially enjoyed Pearl's somewhat unnecessarily enthusiastic praise at how quickly – in her eyes – I'd mastered it.

'That's amazing. Nobody has ever got it that fast. You're a natural, Alice.'

I glowed, and flipped the switches and plugged in the plugs with even greater panache.

'Officer Stevens? Mrs Stevens for you, sir. Mrs Stevens? Thank you for waiting Mrs Stevens. You're through, Mrs Stevens. Officer Stevens, Mrs Stevens for you.'

'She'll be wanting you to fetch her a loaf for him to take home.' Pearl correctly predicted. Mrs S – or Edna Betty, as we usually referred to her – only ever rang in the late afternoon and always to ask if he'd bring home a round sliced milk loaf from Wimbushes Bakery, and I would be despatched to fetch it. That makes it sound a lot simpler than it was: he'd hang up and I'd disconnect him; he'd then ring down and ask to speak to Pearl; I'd put him through to her desk; he'd ask her to ask me to fetch the loaf; and she'd then relay the request to me, fishing the exact change out of her petty cash box and noting it in the small red book she kept for that purpose. That Mrs Stevens could have asked me straight out seemed not to occur to any of the players in this time-wasting little drama. But then, as it became clear as I went on working there, there was very little to do in that office anyway. The whole thing could probably have been handled by one half-time officer, with possibly one very part-time clerical person. But that's not how councils ran things in those days.

On my first morning Pearl took me to see several other council offices in various parts of Westfield, introducing me to the senior secretary in each one, all of whom were, she said, '*lovely* friends' to her and forever concerned about her health and welfare. After the tour she agreed with me that our offices were far and away the best. Some of the other offices had been in dirty old prefabs or on a back corridor in the council building, whilst we were housed in a large and handsome Victorian semi that had been adapted for the purpose. The three bedrooms upstairs were pleasant roomy offices for the three security officers (Stevens, Park and Hampton); the downstairs lounge was the conference room, complete with tiny kitchen; and the other downstairs room was our office, approached along an opaque glass corridor so we could hear and see people coming, but not be seen ourselves. This meant, Pearl informed me happily and conspiratorially, that we could knit when we weren't busy (which was most of the time) because we'd have ample time to drop the knitting into a desk drawer and start shuffling some papers on our desks. She stressed the importance of keeping 'meaningful papers' on our desks at all times.

That first morning she also bought me a teach-yourself-touch-typing book, as Officer Stevens had made it a condition of my employment that I would learn typing and shorthand so that I could substitute for Pearl whenever she was away. She said she '*just knew*' I'd pick it up very quickly and would soon be as good a typist as she was. She took me to the local college to enrol in night school two evenings a week, beaming with pride as she introduced me. Quite why she was so impressed with me escaped me, but it was a pleasant, and unusual experience for me.

It wasn't a hard job at all; it was fun. We weren't even responsible for keeping our own office clean. An elderly lady named Mrs Wilson, who lived in a wing attached to the back of the house, cleaned the whole place from attic to cellar every night of the working week. Our office was very cosy with a gas fire brought to life every morning by Mrs Wilson, and from time to time various sales reps or delivery people would call in and stay for a chat. There was also a handyman in the cellar – Bill Morris – who changed light bulbs, mended broken things, emptied our waste paper baskets every evening and painted the walls and woodwork inside and out. We had an hour and a half for lunch – Pearl always went home – closed at half past five and we each, separately, had one Saturday in three off.

I learned office-correspondence-speak: inst., ult., penult., etc., foolscap and quarto. In reality, observing and learning the formalities of the business world occupied more of my time than doing any actual office work. And all, as my mother said, good experience for my future careers in the business world.

I never really knew what they did up there in their spacious and quite decently furnished offices. It wasn't 'security' in the sense that they looked after things like locks and the physical safety of council staff. They seemed to be either planning for or preventing some massive disaster that might (or might not) occur in the town or even the county. They regularly worked together on a sort of 'what-if/then what?' paper, which was submitted tremulously by Officer Stevens to the head of the council, after which he would agonise for days until he got word that his efforts had been acceptable. I presume they started on the next one then. As far as I know, these offerings were never rejected. Nor were their practice drill plans ever implemented, though they were updated on an almost weekly basis. Parkinson's Law about work expanding to fill the time available was alive and very well indeed in our office.

In between making tea and coffee, answering the phone and typing envelopes, Pearl and I chatted and got to know each other. She told me about living at home with her elderly irascible mother and how they both adored her much younger brother who was at university, studying pharmacy, though he'd always wanted to be a vicar. I told her about my disaster at the Swansea orphanage and she was sweetly sympathetic and told me how *glad* she was that it had turned out that way because now I was with her, but so *sorry* I'd had to go through all that angst. She was solicitous about my bronchitis – 'I wish I could have come over and looked after you,' and told me how she'd suffered from asthma and bronchitis all her life and nearly died several times, but was much healthier now. She also told me how heartbroken she'd been that my predecessor Pauline had left to get married and moved to Liverpool and had been afraid the shock of it would cause her asthma to return. 'It does that, you know, it can come back when a person has had a bad shock.' I hadn't known that, but nodded solemnly to show I was completely in tune with her and what she was saying.

'We were *that* close,' she said, holding her hand in the air with her middle finger pressed on top of her index one. 'We often finished each other's sentences and *never* had a disagreement. I called her Polly; nobody else called her that – it was our special nickname. She saw you when you came for the interview, you know, and she said, "that's the one!" and she was *right*. She didn't like Linda—the other girl—and was ever so pleased when she backed out to take the library job. Just think, Alice, if she hadn't, you wouldn't be here and I'd be stuck with a junior I knew Polly didn't like. I don't think that would have been good for me at all. I see God's hand in all this. Do you have a strong faith, Alice?'

I think that was the first time I became aware of the need to be what I perceived the other – in this case Pearl – wanted me to be, and I could see I had a lot to live up to, so I didn't hesitate. 'Oh yes. I don't go to church every week, but God is very important to me, Pearl.' I vowed to do better in that department from now on.

'Oh, I'm so pleased. God is very much in my life you know. Simon – my brother – wanted to be a vicar, but it couldn't happen. He worries so much about me; my health is permanently on his prayer list. I'm so proud of him. You'll meet him soon; he's coming home over the Easter break. And bringing his friend Henry, I think. Henry will be a vicar and he looks after Simon's spiritual health. They're very good friends as well as spirit-souls.'

Pearl told me about the upstairs staff. There was Officer Park who was, Pearl informed me, 'quite common really' and whose son would fairly regularly run away from home. Sure enough, 'He's gone again,' Mr Park would come into our office every two or three weeks and growl, as we did our best to display sympathy and not collapse into giggles. Officer Hampton was unremittingly cheerful, singing out 'All well?' on his way upstairs to his own sanctum, and given to using the expressions 'as it were' and 'to a degree' a lot, phrases neither Pearl nor I had ever heard before and were not entirely sure of their meanings. Pearl thought he had a bit of class, but probably not as much as me. Class was very important to Pearl and I could see she struggled to find my spot on her scale, but because she liked me I got the nod and went above Mr Hampton. Chief Officer Stevens was below Hampton, and above Mr Park, having 'made something of himself', although he was 'let down', Pearl said, by Edna Betty's common streak. I don't know where Pearl put herself; possibly above Mr Stevens but below Mr Hampton. Certainly below me; I was at the top. She loved the way I said 'tour' (rhyming with door), she said; she pronounced it 'two-uh' in typical Westfield area of Midlands dialect that would have set my mother's teeth on edge.

Mostly, of course, I talked about Jack. Pearl was a romantic (she told me so, more than once) and was satisfyingly interested in all I had to say about him. I didn't exactly invent the romantic things he'd said or done, but I did dress them up quite a bit... and increasingly found myself wishing Jack was as I was portraying him. She definitely wasn't impressed that we called each other Spud; that was not a romantic or even acceptable thing to call your girlfriend, according to Pearl. 'He should call you darling, darling Alice.' (I didn't think he knew the word actually.) It was important to me that she admired him, so instead of telling her that he worked in a furniture factory, I said he was a craftsman carpenter and had, in fact, worked on the lovely carved doors she could find at the front of the church at the top end of Westfield. This gross exaggeration (in reality he'd helped hang them) not only raised him a notch on her class-scale, but also, by some bizarre remote extension, moved him into the God-is-in-my-life arena: 'Oh, such a *Godly* thing to do, Alice. Michelangelo did such lovely paintings in the Sistine Chapel. Have you ever seen the Sistine Chapel, Alice?'

I didn't tell Pearl about our heavy necking sessions on the sofa. I came close once, hinting at it to gauge her reaction, but quickly realised the danger when she said, 'You know, Alice, women can't have satisfactory sex lives after they're married if they go too far before then. They are never able to have organisms.' I hadn't known that; and actually I didn't know what she meant by organisms (I wouldn't have known then if she'd used the correct word, either) but I did know that Pearl would not approve of what Jack and I were doing, and I was enjoying her obvious approbation of me far too much to risk spoiling it any sooner than I had to. It would probably happen eventually; I would inevitably, as my mother often said, wear out my welcome, because 'a little of you goes a long way,' but the longer I could put it off, the better.

THREE

Nobody had ever been so positively warm towards me as Pearl was, not even Jack. The most he could manage in the way of an endearment was some variation of a kind of potato: 'my crispy little roast King Edward' was one of his better efforts to date, but just plain 'Spud' was more usual. I had not been very popular at school, and at home I always felt I was somehow a disappointment and a failure. In fact, 'I'm disappointed in you, Alice' was something I heard from my mother quite a lot, along with the aforementioned 'a little of you goes a long way, so don't outstay your welcome', comment. One difficulty was that I wasn't a boy, like my brilliant and ever-successful (even when he was failing) older brother. My mother really only liked males and although I did my best and behaved as tomboyishly as I could, it wasn't enough. In fact it was entirely wrong; if she *had* to have a girl, then it turned out that she wanted a dainty and feminine one. Not a lumpen hoyden – another of her not very secretly held opinions of me.

My father didn't like anyone except himself, so I'd mostly given up trying to please him. The main objective for a long time had been to stay out of his way and this was now surprisingly easy: he was up and off to his job as warehouse manager for an old friend's factory before I appeared (I told Pearl he was a 'time and motion study' expert) and he was glued to the television in the snug with my mother (he to criticise, she to enjoy despite that) when I got home to eat my solitary dinner in the kitchen, after which I'd either educate myself by listening to classical music on the kitchen radio, or hunker down in bed with a mind-improving book, or, once or twice a week and every weekend, spend a sweaty hour or so on the lounge sofa with Jack. A nice and entirely satisfactory mix, I felt.

I was horribly conflicted about our sessions. I loved Jack desperately and was greatly aroused by our physical grapplings and longed for a time we could legitimately 'go all the way'. But I was terrified of getting pregnant and the inevitable disappointment that would bring from my mother, as well as the scorn and shame from everyone who knew me.

Jack never mentioned marriage so I didn't dare count on that to rescue me, should the worst happen. I was fortunate enough to have very regular periods, so my anxiety each month was quite short-lived and based on no late period evidence. But the anxiety was ever there, nonetheless.

We took terrible risks. For starters we would both be completely naked (with my parents in bed right above our heads) and Jack would stroke his penis all over my labia and sometimes even push it a tiny way in. I would then tense up and push him away so he would get on his knees astride me at my waist and I would press my ample breasts together to make a cleavage for him to thrust into until he ejaculated, moaning things like 'Oh Spud, oh my crunchy little baked potato dripping with butter' as he did so. There was no way I could talk about this to Pearl. I wouldn't have known what words to use anyway. I certainly wasn't going to tell her what he said, and in any case, I was horribly ignorant and hadn't even known before dating Jack that men have 'organisms'. (I did look that up in the office dictionary when Pearl was at lunch and when it didn't enlighten me at all, I looked at nearby words and eventually found the right one. I felt very superior to Pearl by now knowing the word orgasm, and prayed that her ignorance extended to her being completely wrong about the dangers of pre-marital messing about.) Jack might have been reassuring, but I never felt able to bring up the topic of sex with him. We never actually discussed what we did, which is amazing when it was such an important part of our relationship.

Normal physiological happenings were so shaming to talk about that once, early in our relationship, when I desperately needed to pee on our way home from the pub, I couldn't bring myself to tell him, so I rushed to the loo as soon as we got home. When I came out I told him I'd been sick, rather than confess (as I saw it) to what had actually happened. In any case, he was not concerned; he had other things on his mind. After pulling me down to sit on his lap, he put my hand on his penis, fished in his pocket for his rather grubby handkerchief, and ejaculated with a series of joyous whoops. I hadn't known what was happening, but did we talk about it? We did not. After a bit of post-coital kissing he cleaned himself up, said,

'See you tomorrow, my luscious little mashed potato pie', and left.

Most of my sex education theory came from my school friend Pat who clearly had masses of working knowledge on the subject of French kissing, snogging, frigging and various other activities that didn't seem to have names, polite or otherwise. Pat was vastly superior to me in experience and not particularly kind about my ignorance. So I did a lot of nodding sagely and wondered where I could look these things up. I didn't think I could ask the dried-up prune lady in the local library for a reference book and obviously this was not a topic I could bring up with Miss Pearl Taylor, a 35-year-old spinster. In any case, she'd already made her views on this subject clear.

What I did manage to bring up though, was her own past. One day, and never expecting the answer I got, I asked, crassly, 'How about you, Pearl? Don't tell me love has passed you by?'

She slumped over her typewriter and dropped the two-ply black cardigan she was knitting for brother Simon (who wanted to be a vicar but was going to be a pharmacist) into the middle drawer.

'Oh no... no, not at all. No, Alice, my Love was killed five years ago.' Her chin sank to her chest and her shoulders drooped. One of her cheap-looking earrings slipped off its mooring and landed in her lap.

'Oh Pearl! Oh God I'm so sorry. How *awful* for you.' I had no idea how to be or what to say, but she seemed to be waiting for *something*. It crossed my mind that perhaps I was supposed to go over to her and hug her, but I shoved the thought aside and stayed firmly at my desk 'How? I mean, what happened? If you want to tell, that is...'

'Oh I do, I do want to tell you, Alice. He was killed in an air crash. He was a test pilot for the RAF, he used to be in the RAF you see, and the plane he was taking out for a test flight went wrong.'

'Oh my goodness, Pearl....'

15

'He could have bailed out and saved himself, but then the plane would have crashed into a built-up area so he stayed in and guided it into a safe place to crash. So he was killed. On the first of December 1953. Killed, saving countless others' lives. But no, Alice, I'm not resentful about that. I wouldn't have it any other way.' She nodded her head up and down, her mouth set in a hard straight line and her other earring wobbling dangerously.

I stared at her, having no idea of the right thing to do or say. Evidently my riveted attention was enough for now, and she continued.

'We were going to announce our engagement that weekend. He'd told his parents and they were thrilled for us, but he wanted to formally ask my mother. She didn't know about him, you see. She's a very selfish woman and never likes me having any kind of life of my own.'

'Does she know now he's... that he was...?'

'No, there wasn't any point telling her.' She picked up her earring and screwed it more or less back where it belonged. 'She'd never have been able to comfort me so I just kept it all to myself. I haven't even told Simon. Only Cyril and his family knew about us. Till now, and now *you* know. I'm glad you know, Alice. It's a comfort to me to be able to talk to you about him.'

I was beyond staggered. I'd never met anyone with such a horror story. I thought of how ghastly it would be if something happened to Jack and I couldn't talk to my mother about it. We had our differences, my mum and me, but I'd still want to tell her something of this magnitude and I'm pretty sure she would have somehow managed to be at least a bit of a comfort. Pearl seemed not to have told Polly about it, either, if only Cyril's family knew. How on earth had Pearl survived such a thing? I asked her.

'I thought I wouldn't. It brought my asthma back in full force – after more than ten years of being clear. But God never sends you more than you can bear Alice, and Cyril's family – the Brownes, with an e – have been very good to me. His mother wrote me the most exquisite letter very soon after it happened and I treasure that. Knowing her grief must have been something awful, too. Your children aren't supposed to die before you, you know – it's not in the order of things. We're still in touch, and his sister, she stays in touch to make sure I'm all right.' She sighed, 'They worry about me such a lot.'

I didn't know what to say. Unfortunately (or fortunately; I think I was more than a little relieved) Chief Officer Stevens rang down for Pearl to go up for dictation. It was late in the afternoon, so when she returned she hurriedly typed the two letters so I could do the envelopes and get them into that evening's post on my way to catch my bus.

As I was leaving she said, after blowing her nose rather wetly, 'Oh Alice, I'm so glad I've told you about Cyril. Thank you so much for listening and for your lovely, healing sympathy.'

Whilst she'd been upstairs, and later on the bus home, my mind chewed over the story. I struggled to block out the thought that it was too fantastic for words. I think it was the bit about him guiding the plane away from the built-up area so as not to kill dozens of other people that was perhaps one detail too far. And *Cyril!* Who names their kid Cyril? Well, obviously the Brownes (with an e) do. Or did.

I told my mother about it when I got home. We seemed to be getting on better these days than we had, possibly because I was now respectably employed in a job she approved of and that I liked and hadn't failed in. At least not yet.

I tried to be fairly neutral when I told her Pearl's story, partly because I hadn't really wanted to think the unthinkable but also because I wanted to get her untainted reaction. If anything, I went a bit the other way and told her the saga in an oh-ain't-it-awful way.

She went in a different direction though. 'When women of her age have a bad experience with love they become a bit odd. They can get all twisted and bitter.'

I thought about that. Pearl didn't seem twisted and bitter. Did she seem 'odd'? I didn't explore that too deeply, but pondered on the likelihood of an ex-RAF test pilot falling in love with her at age thirty or so. (I was still only seventeen, so anybody over about twenty-two was too old for romance in my opinion.) She wasn't pretty and I didn't think she ever had been. She'd told me she used to be fat, but her illness had caused her to lose a lot of weight. Perhaps she'd looked better then. Now her hands were thin and bony with claw-like fingers on which an unpleasant-looking marquisate ring dangled precariously, and her mouth was frankly nauseating to me with its soft and saggy lower lip that always looked wet. She was thin, but not in a shapely way, and her neck was what they called crepey as far down as I could see. Not that I really looked – in fact, I tried not to look too hard at her – I found her quite repulsive.

FOUR

Next morning, feeling mean about my uncharitable thoughts, I stopped on my way to the office to buy Pearl a small bunch of snowdrops from the little newspaper-cum-florist shop at the bus station. She was, predictably, over-the-top thrilled, very nearly making me regret my impulse. If my mother felt a little of *me* went a long way, I thought, she should try spending half a day with Pearl.

'Oh Alice! Oh what a darling you are. *Nobody* has bought me flowers since Cyril and he never bought me snowdrops because he wasn't here with me, in my life, in the snowdrop season, of course. I've always loved snowdrops, and so did he, I knew that. They mean so much, they are such a promise of better things to come, don't you think?'

Yes, I suppose so, is what I thought, but 'Oh yes, definitely,' is what I said.

For the next two weeks it was a nonstop Cyril-fest. She told me how they'd met – in what Hollywood calls a 'meet cute' of course – in the doctor's waiting room apparently: she with a bad case of bronchitis and struggling to breathe and he for some necessary inoculation or other. He'd insisted on her taking his turn and then, finishing before her, had waited for her and driven her home. She'd demurred, of course, but he hadn't taken no for an answer, making her wait in the surgery till he brought the car to the door. An Alvis tourer– very fitting for an RAF test pilot from a posh family with money.

'Didn't your mother notice you arriving in a car instead of walking?' I was already fact checking. Or just being difficult? I couldn't imagine anyone, let alone a 'handsome RAF test pilot' finding Pearl, or anybody else with a streaming cold and wracking cough, attractive. And I couldn't imagine that an Alvis tourer wouldn't attract quite a bit of attention in her fairly working-class neighbourhood, either.

'She didn't see. I made him let me out before we got to our gate. He didn't want to, of course, he wanted to see me safely right to the door, but I wouldn't let him. I didn't want to face my mother's probing questions you see. I was too ill. Cyril knew that.'

I learned about their first date – he'd resourcefully taken note of her address and written to ask how she was and if she'd like to go with him to see the Merry Widow at the Royal in Birmingham next week, if she was better. Which he hoped she was.

'Didn't your mother ask who your letter was from?' God, I was annoying, and struggling not to wonder why the RAF doctor as opposed to the local GP couldn't have given him the required inoculation.

'Fortunately she was busy – doing the washing up – when the post came so she didn't know I had it. When I replied I asked him to contact me only at the office after that. Oh just think, Alice, if you'd been here then you'd have been answering the phone to him.'

'Hmm.'

She told me about him buying her chocolates on their way in and then reaching for a chocolate from the box on her lap during the second act, and taking her hand instead. She told me how they'd heard Sibelius's Finlandia together (presumably at another time) and how she'd never been able to hear it since because it became 'their' piece of music. She told me about meeting his lovely family who lived in the posh part of Westfield of course, and how she now had the sister she'd always wanted: Marjorie ('never Marge') Browne with an e, now Mrs Angus McIntosh. Somewhat to my relief, I didn't have to hear about their first kiss – they were saving that moment for the day they announced their engagement. But I listened with interest, trying hard not to see any discrepancies in the tales. I really wanted it to be true. It was all so romantic, even the fact that they shook hands at the end of their dates together. Imagine if I'd offered to shake Jack's hand instead of an entirely different piece of his anatomy!

'Didn't you at least *want* to hug him, Pearl? Or kiss him?'

'Oh yes, just the touch of his hand was like an electric shock going through me,' she smiled dreamily. 'But you see, Alice, it's not good to do too much physical touching before you're actually married; it can spoil things for later.' God, I hoped she was wrong about that. I preferred to believe Jack who often said, about the 'real' act of intercourse, 'if God made anything better He certainly kept it to Himself.'

The torrent slowed somewhat when my birthday rolled round. Pearl made a tremendous fuss over me, bringing me a huge slice of coffee cake from home and giving me a nice little copy of Palgrave's *Golden Treasury* that was somewhat spoilt by her sickly inscription on the title page: *To darling Alice on her birthday. I thank God for your birth and that you've come into my life. Love for always, Pearl'.*

I tried not to be irritated by the switch from 'her' to 'your', knowing that my mother would certainly comment on this, and I would be unsure of how I wanted to respond. I didn't like my mother criticising my friends; she knew this and regularly complimented me on my loyalty—and I think I probably realised at the time that she wasn't really meaning this as a positive thing.

Jack gave me some jewellery: a garish purple paste affair comprising necklace, bracelet and earrings, none of which I ever comfortably wore. I wasn't a jewellery person but willed myself to be thrilled because Jack had gone out and bought it for me. (He probably hadn't. He'd probably got one of his numerous sisters to do it for him – and it might have been intended for Wendy Freeman anyway.) But I raved over it to Pearl, already aware that I was reinventing Jack on a daily basis to keep him high in the romantic stakes. He could never come close to Cyril – who could? – but I needed him to be better than he was, and buying me cheap and nasty paste jewellery was not a good start. I half-floated the idea that the stones were genuine amethysts, but Pearl shot that down so quickly that I wasn't even sure she heard what I was trying to say. Mind you, I liked the ensemble better than I liked Pearl's ghastly ring, and at least my earrings stayed on.

His best present to me, which I obviously couldn't tell Pearl about, was my very own 'organism' – my first, and with him, alas, my only. As my birthday was on a Saturday we'd gone as usual to the weekly dance in a nearby town. Because it was my birthday, I expected Jack to pay extra attention to me, and dance in a more erotic way, but it didn't happen. We left fairly early, stopping in the pub for a while and then Jack took me home as usual on the back of his motorbike. My parents were already in bed so we settled onto the sofa for my birthday snog. Already highly aroused, it took very little fingering of my throbbing bits to produce the most amazing feeling all over my body. In hindsight I think he'd found my clitoris accidentally because he never found it again. I'm quite sure neither of us knew it existed. He may have had a hazy notion, but I was completely ignorant. And even if I'd known what word to look up, I'm pretty certain it wouldn't have been in the office dictionary.

The Cyril saga took another back seat when brother Simon and friend Henry called in to visit us. Pearl knew they were coming and went to great lengths to set up a warm welcome, as well as to make sure we were able to look *very* busy. She found some old financial sheets to put on my desk and told me to mention 'calculating emollients' in front of 'my boys'. She put a piece of paper in her typewriter and made sure she was clacking away when they appeared in our glass corridor.

I was mildly disappointed in Simon. He was better looking than Pearl, but still a bit on the weedy side. I wasn't really looking for a replacement for Jack, but it had occurred to me that being a pharmacist's wife had more cachet than being married to a man who worked in a furniture factory. Henry was better looking with nice tight curly iron-grey hair, but closer to fifty than Simon's twenty-five, which surprised me. He paid little attention to me and less to Pearl, seeming to look anywhere but at her. They stayed a very short time, hurrying off when Pearl suggested I might make us all a cup of tea. I hadn't even had time to look at my financial papers, let alone talk about their column headings.

If Pearl noticed their lack of warmth and enthusiasm she didn't show it to me. In fact, she pronounced their visit a great success and just *knew* they had been very impressed with us and our efficiency. 'They didn't want to interrupt our work you see, so they left quickly.'

I didn't know what to say but felt something was expected so, 'They seem to get along well, don't they?'

'Oh yes, but it isn't Simon's friendship that brings Henry home with him.'

'Oh?' I thought I knew what was coming.

'It's me,' sighed Pearl. I was right.

'Don't you like him?' I thought she could do a lot worse and would probably make an excellent vicar's wife.

'I do, he's very nice, but I'm afraid he's working up to asking me to marry him and I can't. There's only ever been one for me, Alice. I could never be unfaithful to Cyril's memory.' She twisted her ring round and round her middle finger.

I didn't know what to say to that except that standard British response to anything emotional: 'I'll make us some tea.'

In quiet moments – like on the bus home – I knew there was a change in my attitude towards Pearl; I no longer automatically believed everything she said without question, but I started being protective of her with other people. It was fine for me to privately sneer at her weirdness, but I didn't like others doing it and felt guilty when I indulged in laughing at her with Pat. My mother told me that my father had said she was a 'pansy without a stalk', which, after some thought, I took to mean he thought she was a lesbian. Mum stuck by her belief that women of 'a certain age' who'd been disappointed in love invariably went slightly batty, so I stopped giving her details of Pearl's latest stories. I did go on a bit about how awful Pearl's mother was to her but stopped even that when my mother said,

'Well, maybe she's hard work to live with. What does she want with you, anyway? She's old enough to be *your* mother.'

I'm not sure if I was protecting Pearl or myself, but when I went to bed that night I carefully tore out and destroyed the title page of my Palgrave's *Golden Treasury* on which Pearl had written her extravagant and fulsome birthday wishes. I enjoyed the book a lot more after that.

Jack, on the other hand, was downright crude about her. 'She wants a good rogering, Spud; there's nowt wrong with 'er that a bloody good shag wouldn't put right.'

I was going off Jack a bit. He only had two jokes and told them regularly: 'Did you hear about the frustrated duck that couldn't get up for down?' and '…then there was the dumb blonde who thought "wriggle it in" was corrugated sheeting'. His grammatical failures were getting on my nerves and his laissez faire table manners often made me cringe. The fact that he didn't seem to know enough – or couldn't be bothered – to put his knife and fork together when he'd finished eating irritated me beyond all reason. I was also secretly offended by his name, which seemed to me – when you compared it with posh names like Cyril and Henry, for example – a bit of a labourer's name. It ought to have been short for John, or James (both reasonably classy names) but it wasn't. He'd simply been named Jack and I didn't like it; it was, in my mother's parlance, common. I don't think I was infected by Pearl's snobbishness; truthfully, I think it was already in place before I ever met her.

Even our steamy sofa sessions had lost their lustre. Jack never again found the right spot to give me an orgasm; I really don't think he knew it was there because if he did accidentally touch on it, he didn't stay on it long enough to make anything happen. I tried shifting my position to maintain contact in what felt like the right place, but he, probably thinking I was uncomfortable, simply moved his fingers elsewhere. Sometimes when he was doing his thing between my breasts – and I was getting a bit fed up with that, too; it did nothing for me – I'd ponder on just how I could put into words what I wanted him to do. I never did though, partly because really I didn't know what words to use, but mostly out of shame. Sex might be something you *do,* but 'nice' people never talked about it.

He started making oblique references to our future together, though he still didn't actually mention marriage. 'We'll have a nice little car instead of the motorbike', and

'Wharton would be a good place to bring the kids up, Spud', and things like that. I hadn't responded; I was desperately afraid I was falling out of love with him. The Jack I talked about with Pearl got less and less like the Jack I was spending three or four evenings a week with, but I was quite heartened when out of the blue he told me he'd read all Shakespeare's works. I couldn't wait to pass that on to Pearl.

'What's his favourite play, Alice?' she wanted to know, so I asked him.

'I didn't like none of 'em,' was his inaccurate reply.

'Why did you read them, then?'

'I wanted to know what all the fuss was about, that's all. Couldn't see it myself.'

I couldn't decide whether this was a good indicator on the 'intelligent, educated and posh' scale or not, so I let the whole matter drop. Not having read more than the required Henry V at school I didn't really feel I was qualified to comment anyway. I also suspected he hadn't really understood them any more than I had.

A Very Bad Thing on the scale though was a visit to his family one Saturday afternoon. They were very definitely not what my mother would have called 'our kind of people', and I'm pretty sure they didn't take to me any better than I took to them. His wizened little father sat scrunched in a tiny battered armchair about three feet from the coal fire into which he spat at irregular intervals. His mother, doing the ironing around the salt and sugar packets and milk bottle on a vast table that almost filled the room, launched into a seemingly endless tale about how her youngest daughter, Jack's little sister, had just started her 'monthlies' and hadn't known what was happening. For all my sexual ignorance, I'd been well prepared for *that* event and had greatly looked forward to its arrival, but I tried to seem interested in the saga. I'm not sure it made any difference though; I think his mother would have gone on and on no matter how I'd responded. She seemed proud of the fact that she hadn't given any 'grown-up' information to her baby girl. The sister in question wasn't there, and I wondered how she'd feel at being the topic of this particular conversation. She was probably used to it.

Jack spent the entire afternoon in their shed, dismantling his motorbike with one or other of his several brothers. I went out to chat to them for a while, but this isn't how they do it in their family: the women stay indoors and do women things and the men go out to the shed and do man things. And never the twain shall meet, apparently – unless she's taking him a cup of tea and a handful of custard creams. He and the brothers essentially ignored me for twenty minutes so I went unhappily back inside, wondering how long it would take me to walk home. Mrs Watson seemed not to have noticed my absence and was still in full flight with her unpleasant story of daughter Susan's first attack of the monthlies.

When the bike was reassembled and Jack finally took me home on it I didn't let him come in. He was a bit shocked, but acquiesced easily enough and left, promising to see me again tomorrow. I went to bed with a sense of freedom and wondered what it would be like to say no to him tomorrow when he wanted us to get stuck in to our usual Sunday evening occupation. Maybe I'd go to church instead.

FIVE

There seemed to be no more Cyril stories (*could* there be anything else – they'd only been together for a couple of months) but that didn't stop Pearl, the self-described romantic. But Henry – and his desire to marry Pearl – reappeared. He was, Pearl told me, coming for the weekend, without Simon this time, and she was absolutely convinced he was going to declare his love for her and ask for her hand in marriage (that's actually how she phrased it, too).

'Have you ever been out on a date with him, Pearl?' I couldn't work out how she'd arrived at her conviction of his undying passion for her. I may be a bit naïve, but I thought I would have seen *something* when he and Simon came to our office.

'No... well, not... no, we haven't actually been *out.*'

'Have you even spent much time alone with him? What's that been like?' I knew she didn't like the questions, but if she was asking for my help I had to know what I was getting in to. 'How many times has he been to stay with you?'

'Oh two, no, more, maybe three or four... Maybe less. Mother and Simon have always been there, of course, but you *know* Alice, I just *know*... I don't want to hurt him, Alice, but I don't know what to do or what to say. You're so good with words, what do *you* think I should say?'

Years of reading Mary Grant's Problem Page in *Woman's Own* had not been wasted: 'Well, if you're sure you don't want to marry him I think you've got two options. You can wait until he asks you and say you're ever so sorry, but there'll never be anyone but Cyril for you, or you can launch a pre-emptive strike and announce to all and sundry that you'll never marry because you'll never get over Cyril. That seems a better way to me, actually; Henry doesn't have to make a fool of himself then.'

'Oh Alice, you're really brilliant! Thank you so much. I'll do that, at supper, I'll find a way to say something like that and that'll help him save face, too. That's important for men, you know.'

With great relief I went to make our morning coffee, hoping she wouldn't come up with another 'what if...?' and start the whole conversation again.

But no, she was ready to move on: 'Have I ever told you about Cyril's sister, Marjorie, and how she met her husband, Alice?'

Another 'meet cute', this time at the dentist. Marjorie (never Marge) had had the most awful toothache and the dentist she had seen since she was a child was away: somewhere exotic, naturally. She, terrified of dentists, had tried to suffer on, waiting for him to return, but in the end had had to give in and see his new, young and handsome assistant, Mr McIntosh. And he, in the course of reassuring and comforting her – as well as taking out her rotten tooth – had fallen in love with her immediately: 'with blood and pus running down her chin and tears streaming from her eyes', Pearl elaborated.

'Angus made her keep coming back for follow-up appointments long after she was all healed up, just so he could see her again.' In the end he'd plucked up the nerve to ask her out and apparently they never looked back from there. They'd been married only two years and were desperately trying to have a baby before they hit forty.

Despite myself, I was enthralled. 'Did you go to the wedding, Pearl?'

'Oh no. They were married in Scotland – all in a swirl of kilts and sporrans and bagpipes. I was invited of course, and they would have paid for me to go up there and for my hotel, but they completely understood that I couldn't do it. Her mother said how hard it was for her that Cyril wasn't there. ''He should have been best man and you should have been the matron of honour'' she kept saying. It was so hard for her that we weren't there, but I couldn't do it. I would have broken down completely.'

Hating myself: 'And you couldn't leave your mother, either.'

Pearl sagged another inch or two. 'No… that would have presented difficulties.'

Hating myself even more: 'Wouldn't the best man have been a friend of Angus though?'

'Well, of course it *was*, but he loved the idea of having Cyril if Cyril hadn't… if he had lived.'

Tears seemed likely, so I changed tack. 'You'll have to bring in the photos; I'd love to see them. And photos of Cyril, too – I'd love to see what he looks like.'

Pearl didn't answer and I wondered if any photographs actually existed. Friend Pat said, when I told her this latest saga, 'Well, how could they exist, when Cyril and Marge don't?'

It was suspicious, but Pat was convinced, so when the phone rang towards the end of the lunch break a few days later I became confused all over again.

'Westfield Council Security Office, Miss Chorley speaking. May I help you?' As it wasn't yet half past two and I was technically still at lunch, I hadn't been required to respond, but I had nothing else to do, so I answered it anyway.

'Miss Taylor, please.' It could have been anybody but it was definitely a Westfield and environs accent aiming to be posh, and I thought it came from a phone box.

'I'm afraid she's at lunch until half past two. May I give her a message?'

'This is Mrs McIntosh. Just tell her I rang, if you will.'

'Would you like her to ring you back, Mrs McIntosh?' Calmly, but inside I was humming with excitement. This was *Marjorie*!

'No, I won't be here. I'm ringing from a phone box, actually, and I won't be home until much later. Just tell her I rang please.'

'Certainly, Mrs McIntosh. Goodbye.'

Pearl arrived ten minutes later. 'You'll never guess who rang for you, Pearl,' I burbled.

Pearl looked quizzically at me. 'Who?'

'Your sister! Well, sort of sister-in-law, really; Mrs McIntosh, no less.'

'Oh Alice! Is she all right? What did she say? Did you talk to her? Tell me, tell me…'

So I did. I repeated the boring business-like conversation as word for word as I could remember. Pearl just nodded and spent most of the rest of the afternoon telling me how lovely Marjorie was and how happy she and Angus were. Except that she seemingly couldn't get pregnant. Presumably they were having a marvellous time trying, though. In fact, Pearl said they did, affecting a stomach-churning coyness as she did so.

Unfortunately, the more Pearl told me about Marjorie and Angus, the harder it was to ignore my growing sense that Jack wasn't enough for me. I wanted – needed! – a man with a bit more class, a man I wouldn't be ashamed to introduce to people like the McIntoshes, for instance. And I needed my man to be a lot more romantic and understanding than poor Jack would ever manage. And preferably with a family I could warm to. I struggled with my feelings, praying as hard as I could that if God would just grant me six months of loving and feeling loved by Jack, I'd settle for whatever happened after that. As hard as it was to consider a future with him, I couldn't bear the idea of an immediate future without him.

God in His wisdom did not give me six months of happiness. He didn't actually manage much more than about six seconds of conviction that Jack was the right one for me. Instead, and try as I did to ignore it, I felt that same solid conviction of decision that I'd had about leaving the Swansea orphanage, so when, one evening after bringing me home from the pictures, Jack said, 'I think we'll ask your father tonight, Spud,' I panicked.

'NO! No don't. I'm not sure any more. I can't. I'm sorry. I… I don't think this is right for me after all.' Bizarrely, I flung my arms around his neck, desperately needing him to give me a reassuring hug.

'But you were so *sure,* Spud,' He was understandably gobsmacked. I was horrified at what I'd done, but I was also tremendously relieved and couldn't wait to get him out.

He stayed for a little while, talking about nothing much, and then left. He was kind and dignified, gave me the reassuring hug, and I felt terrible, even though I knew I'd made the right decision. And for the first time for weeks I had no trouble sleeping at all.

I told my mother a few days later and she said she knew, Jack had written a goodbye letter to her. 'Can I see it?'

Horrid little snob that I was, it cemented my decision. He'd written, *'I'm sorry I can't say goodby in pearson'.*

Mum didn't say she was disappointed though. She didn't say she was pleased, that would have been a step too far for her, but at least she wasn't disappointed in me.

Pearl was very pleased. '*I* knew he wasn't good enough for you, but I didn't think *you* knew,' she said, after she'd mouthed the customary sympathies. That shocked me. Why would she think I would want less for myself than she would? Even worse, she apparently hadn't been taken in my stories of how lovely and romantic Jack was, though to her credit, she never said so.

No more Jack meant I now had extra evenings and all weekends free. If Pearl had been allowed out without her mother (they went everywhere together despite, according to Pearl, having the most coruscating arguments pretty much non-stop) we could have gone to the theatre or concerts together, things that Jack had had no interest in at all. Instead she told me what was worth going to and I went alone. Occasionally I would glimpse Pearl and her mother there but she was careful to avoid me if she could.

'Mother is so jealous of my friends, you see. If she thought I liked you or wanted to spend any time with you, she'd hate you and never stop running you down. And I wouldn't be able to bear that.'

Mother did occasionally go away though. Shortly after my parting from Jack she took herself off to North Wales for a week, and Pearl was in heaven.

'I shall wash in the bathroom and sit in the lounge and eat what and when I like – in the dining room if I want to! I can have a bath every night if I feel like it.' Apparently they only ever used their kitchen, including for washing themselves. 'And we can go to the theatre and you can come home with me to stay the night!'

So we did. Pearl could hardly manage her excitement as we walked into the theatre in Wharton, and kept giving annoying little squeaks as she looked at the programme. Still trying to be what I perceived she wanted me to be, I squeezed her hand a couple of times to indicate that I, too, was having a marvellous time. And in a way I was. Pearl was enthusiastic and cheerful company, which contrasted sharply with Jack's habitual lack of conversation and general gloom at whatever was happening. She had kindly bought the tickets so I bought her an ice cream in the interval, bringing forth her usual over-the-top and fulsome praise and gratitude.

'Crikey – it's only a flipping ice cream, Pearl, not the crown jewels.'

'I know, but it's *so* lovely to be with you and having such a pleasant time together. It's the best ice cream I've ever had, because *you* bought it. Oh, how I wish Mother would go away more often; we could do so much together...'

I took the bull by his proverbials. 'Pearl, you should just *tell* your mother you're going out and she's not invited. You're a grown woman, you've got to have a life of your own.'

'I know. I will. I promise. Though you don't know what you're asking, Alice. But for you, I'll try to be stronger.' She spun her much-too-big ring round her bony finger; a habit I'd noticed many times before, and I wondered again if I was supposed to ask where it came from, but I didn't. I didn't really care.

Pearl and her mother lived in a little three-bedroom semi on the outskirts of Westfield. The house had a fairly decent-sized sitting room, a small dining room, three bedrooms and a bathroom upstairs. I assume they both actually used their bedrooms, but downstairs they apparently never went into any rooms other than the mean little kitchen, where they evidently sat hunched over a one-bar electric fire in chairs that had obviously come from the same jumble sale as Jack's father's chair. They washed themselves in the scullery, though Pearl was quick to assure me they each had a bath once a week. Hopefully without sharing the bathwater, but I didn't ask.

'Why? I mean why on earth do you not sit in your sitting room or eat in your dining room? What do you do when you have guests? Do you eat in the kitchen then?' I lived in a large sprawl of a house and could not conceive of us shutting off even one of our many rooms.

Typically, as I was slowly recognising, she ignored the questions she didn't want to answer and just looked downcast for a moment. Then, cheerfully, 'Well, you're here now and we can use the bathroom. So long as we leave it all as it was so Mother doesn't suspect. She mustn't know you've been here. You don't know how difficult she can be, Alice.'

She showed me up to her brother's room – after giving me a guided tour of her own totally Pearl-like sanctuary, filled with icons, religious books, and even a black velvet picture of what I think was supposed to be Christ ascending into Heaven. Sleeping in there night after night would have given me nightmares. God knows what their occasional visitors – like Henry – made of it, for it doubled as the guest room. Apparently poor old rejected Henry had even had to sleep in there on his failed visit earlier that month while Pearl miserably bunked in with her mother. (As promised, Pearl had made her off-putting statement over the sardines on toast and blancmange and custard meal, and Henry had taken it 'bravely' but with tears in his eyes. I rather wished I could have been a fly on the wall for that little scene, though I'd no doubt Pearl exaggerated both her behaviour and Henry's response.)

Simon's room was perfect for a wannabe vicar: small, bare (single bed, chest and chair only) and cold. A crucifix but no pictures on the walls, dirty-brown linoleum on the floor, tiny window overlooking next door's bins, and the most ghastly dull grey and black curtains I'd ever seen. More suitable for an about-to-be a monk, really. Or a pharmacist. I wondered, briefly, why Henry hadn't slept in here, but couldn't be bothered to ask.

I made what I quickly realised was a mistake next morning as Pearl was cooking me a 'proper' breakfast: I answered 'yes, I was actually,' when she asked if I'd been cold in the night.

'Oh poor you! Next time you're coming in with me and we'll keep each other warm.'

SIX

Now that I was no longer making Jack out to be the most romantic man since who knows when, I found myself slightly reinventing my parents; or at least their relationship with each other. After making sure Pearl understood that my father was only doing his business friend a favour by staying on and running the warehouse he'd so lovingly redesigned and systemised, (he wasn't *really* a blue-collar worker; my mother would not have put up with that) I put my fertile imagination to work on their demonstrations of romantic and enduring love for each other.

In reality my father did have his romantic side, but it wasn't something my mother encouraged; possibly because his loving gestures had a tendency to flourish far beyond the boundaries of their relationship. I could easily name (and so could my mother) at least five reasonably attractive middle-aged women in our village who had been the object of his affections at one point or another – some of which were undoubtedly reciprocated. He could be very charming if he felt like it. Unfortunately for his family, his mood was anything but reliable: you'd be jogging along, having a pleasant chat or banter with him when out of the blue – and for absolutely no discernible reason – he'd lose his temper and ruin the moment; as well as many subsequent moments for the next hours or even days. It was behaviour like that that kept me out of his orbit whenever possible.

Like many men who'd served in the war, he had kept his Army issue revolver (nestling cosily in his underwear drawer among the Y-fronts) and my mother was never sure if his threats to 'end it all' were the angry, empty gestures they inevitably turned out to be. Most rows between them – and there were many – culminated in him storming out angrily to walk it off along the canal path and my mother dashing upstairs to reassure herself that the revolver was still there. It always was, and sometimes I'd feel quite sorry that he wasn't going to make good his threat, though I'm not sure he had any bullets anyway. I wouldn't have wanted that for my mother but I couldn't imagine it being anything other than a huge relief to me. And possibly to my brother; there was no love lost between him and his procreator, either. But I absolutely didn't tell Pearl any of this.

I never expected Pearl to meet either of my parents and certainly not to see them together, but her mother went up to Leeds to visit Simon at university and unexpectedly decided to stay for the night. As it was a Monday night and therefore my music appreciation class, I rather recklessly invited Pearl to come with me and to come home afterwards and stay at our house.

It went quite well. She came with me on the bus and we happily frittered away the two hours before the class began with fish and chips from the local chippy and a walk round the cathedral. She was actually quite knowledgeable about its history and was obviously on nodding terms with a couple of the young deans who were walking around whilst we were there. (She really should have married Henry; she'd have made a splendid vicar's wife.) She liked the class and the funny little man who taught us each week, and approved of my (actually quite naïve) questions, and we walked home in unusual but friendly enough silence, each of us re-hearing the music in our head. Well, I was – I don't know what Pearl was doing or thinking about.

The parents were, as usual at that time on a Monday evening, ensconced in the snug with the telly, and – with absolutely no knowledge of the script I'd written for them – behaved impeccably. They made conventional and pleasant conversation with us for a while and then, with somewhat exaggerated yawning, declared themselves ready for bed. You'd never have known my father and I mutually despised one another and that he had hardly spoken to me since I left the Swansea orphanage.

'Right darling, off we go,' said he, taking my mother's hand. He would *never* have done that if he hadn't been showing off for Pearl (or someone, anyone), but I really appreciated it and smiled conspiratorially at her as they left. She loved it. And she loved hearing me say 'Goodnight Daddy, goodnight, Mummy,' as they left, though I tried to say it softly enough for them not to hear me, because I only ever called my mother Mum, and I never called my father anything if I could help it, and certainly not Daddy. But Pearl had often remarked that posh people like Marjorie (and Cyril?) used these what felt to me like childish diminutives. So whenever we talked about my parents in the office, that's how I referred to them, posh child that I was. (I didn't think it was at all upper class for a father not to be speaking to his grown-up daughter, so I hadn't mentioned that to Pearl, either.)

We waited a decent interval for them to use the bathroom, and then I deposited Pearl safely in the spare bedroom, feeling quite proud of my home, my parents, and my posh life. I don't know what came over my mother but, Pearl told me excitedly next morning, she actually went in to say goodnight to my guest. 'She tucked me in,' Pearl confided. 'My mother has never done that.'

My mother hadn't either, in my memory, but something had evidently moved her to a bit of tenderness for poor old Pearl, whose disappointment in love was probably turning her a bit odd. Or possibly she was checking up to make sure my father wasn't in there with some nefarious agenda of his own, though I couldn't imagine that even he would find Pearl in any way alluring. She, of course, went over it and over it for days, weeks, afterwards. 'Your mother is *so loving*, Alice', now became the prelude to a steady stream of Angus and Marjorie anecdotes.

'Marjorie was so nervous on their wedding night that she fainted. When she came round Angus had undressed her and she was completely naked in the bed. And he was so kind. He just lay in the bed, holding her hand, all night long.'

'So no, erm... no, you know...?' I hoped Pearl *did* know what I was asking because I couldn't manage to get the words out. All I could think of was Jack's favourite – shag – and that was definitely not the word to use in connection with Angus and Marjorie.

'Oh no, not for several nights. He wanted her to feel safe and comfortable with him, you see. He knew she was shy,' Pearl sighed and looked out of the window. 'A long time later she asked him why she had been naked and he had been in his pyjamas and do you know what he said?'

I shook my head, rapt.

'He said, "a woman's body is a beautiful thing, but a man's is not". She was so touched, so grateful, and of course that helped her to feel completely and utterly safe with him. It helped her get over her shyness with him, you see.'

I was a bit surprised. I hadn't found Jack's body unbeautiful, not at all. Even so, I found all this very romantic and wanted to hear more, but sometimes in the quiet of the night I wondered if Pearl was telling me more about her own views on sex, men and bodies than either of us quite realised. In daylight hours I continued to believe Angus had behaved beautifully, and I was envious. I wanted just such a man for myself.

Shortly after Pearl's visit home with me, Marjorie rang again. At lunchtime again (and again from a phone box) so our exchange was almost identical to the first time. Until she said, 'Am I speaking to Alice?'

'Yes, this is Alice.'

'Pearl has told me all about you. She thinks the world of you, you know, so I feel I can confide in you a little bit. I hope that's all right, Alice?'

I was thrilled. 'Of course it is. And I think the world of Pearl, too,' I exaggerated.

'I know you do. Of course you do. We all do. And we worry about her so much. She's so brave, so courageous, I'm sure you see that all the time. I'm so lucky and she's had such a horrid time. She's been so ill... And she has so much to put up with at home... we worry about her health terribly and were so relieved to hear what a wonderful friend she has in you.'

I wanted to ask if they hadn't felt the same about my predecessor, but before I could work out how to ask tactfully – I didn't want to seem to be in competition with someone I'd never met and who was no longer even on the scene – Marjorie said, 'May I ring from time to time to make sure she is all right? I wouldn't want to be a nuisance, but Pearl is such a dear, brave soul...' She trailed off with a sigh.

Of course I said of course she could. I was deeply flattered, but also a bit astonished. For one thing, why was she ringing from a phone box and why at lunchtime when she must know Pearl wasn't there. Oh, yes, she wanted to find out how Pearl is from *me*. That's why she rang when she knew Pearl wasn't there. But it didn't explain why she couldn't ask Pearl directly how she was. Nor did it explain the phone box.

As I waited for Pearl to return from lunch, I wondered whether I was supposed to tell her about this call or not. Marjorie hadn't said, one way or the other. It seemed odd to say nothing, but on the other hand, what was there to say? I certainly didn't want to feed her obsession with her own health and how everybody was so concerned about her, by telling her about the arrangement Marjorie had just made with me, though I knew Pearl would absolutely love the idea of it. I heard Officer Hampton come in, with his habitual 'all well?' as he took the stairs two at a time (he never waited for an answer) and then Officer Park arrived at the same time as Pearl and came into our office with her. For a change his 'gone again' son hadn't gone again, but he was still, as usual, the main topic of Park's conversation. We weathered this and then it was time for me to make the tea. Officer Stevens rang for Pearl to do dictation and finally Edna Betty rang to put us through the usual hoops required to get their teatime loaf. By half past five Marjorie's phone call and request for inside information about Pearl seemed a million miles away.

All this is what passed for a busy day in our office. I felt quite tired from it all when I got home.

SEVEN

Part of the attractiveness of friendship with Pearl was that we did share a deep liking for a lot of the important things in my life. Her taste in fiction, for example, often mirrored mine, so when she recommended her latest library book, *The Pilgrim Cottage Omnibus,* I was reasonably sure I would enjoy it, too. It had first been published in 1938 (definitely more her era than mine) but its themes were timeless: boy meets girl, boy falls in love, girl resists at first and then falls heavily... No actual sex, of course, but it was romantic; we both enjoyed that, and I knew we would enjoy discussing it as I read.

Music was another shared pleasure. I was not familiar with a lot of the music Pearl raved over, but in my new life of concert-going and music appreciation classes I was learning fast. I was quite taken by Finlandia, 'their' personal piece of music, so was shocked when Pearl reminded me that she'd never been able to listen to it since Cyril had been killed. She also couldn't listen to, she said, the Sibelius Second Symphony or music from The Merry Widow. In my youthful arrogance, I was determined to do something about that, so when Pearl's thirty-sixth birthday rolled around I bought her a record of Finlandia.

'Oh Alice... I just knew you'd do that,' she gushed, eyes wet and nose dripping nastily. 'I *knew* you'd know that I would be able to listen to it with you.'

I hadn't really bargained for that, but stoically endured her heaving sobs when we put it on the conference room record player next afternoon whilst the officers were all out at a council meeting.

Evidently my silence was just what she needed; I honestly hadn't the faintest idea of what to say, so had said nothing.

'Isn't Sibelius *marvellous?* I think I'm ready to hear his glorious Second now... and even, soon, The Merry Widow', she sniffed bravely.

I gulped. 'That's wonderful, Pearl, but I don't think I can afford....'

'Oh *no*! Of course not. No, no, *I'll* buy them and we can listen together. That's the absolute best present you can give me, ever. Oh Alice, what a wonder you are, how *lucky* I am to have found you.'

I had doubts about my staying power for so much raw emotion during office hours, but felt I must do my best. And true to her word, on our next payday, Pearl trotted straight over to the music shop on the High Street and purchased the lot. I found myself praying hard that there wouldn't be an opportunity to hear them for a long time. I needed time to recover from the last one.

I was doing a fair bit of praying by then, having suddenly embraced religion pretty seriously. I knew this pleased Pearl and whilst I wouldn't admit even to myself that I wanted to please her, I was well aware that I enjoyed impressing her. And she *was* impressed that I went to Holy Communion every day during Holy Week. (I can't say the same for the congregation of my local church who clearly wondered what mischief I was planning *now*. I thought the vicar could have been a bit less sceptical though. After all, he was fairly new on the scene so anything he knew about my past could only have been hearsay.)

But impressing Pearl wasn't my only reason. It really had more to do with God's *not* answering my fervent prayers about not falling out of love with Jack and bargaining for a six month stay of execution. He (God) had obviously known better what was good for me and what would end up being a total disaster. My life had broadened tremendously since my idea of a good time being a session on the sofa with Jack. I was going to a concert or the theatre almost every week, thoroughly enjoying my music appreciation class and actually finding out a lot more about other good things in life. I was grateful for that and so promised God I would try not to bother Him with any more trivial requests if He'd just keep at least one security officer in the building at all times so I didn't have to nurse Pearl through the emotional upheaval of listening to any more of her meaningful music. I pointed out to God that *He* would be much better at providing the necessary comfort than I, an eighteen-year-old flibbertigibbet. He (God) obliged long enough for Pearl to find the courage to listen to her new records at home, and in a rush of gratitude I managed to be graciously understanding when she reported on the experience next day in the office. Pearl said I'd 'listened prayerfully', and whilst I had no idea what she could possibly mean by that, I appreciated her appreciation and was not slow to send my thanks (privately) up to God.

I also appreciated the fact that dealing with Pearl's present emotions seemed slightly more real than listening to her Cyril stories and, for that matter, Angus and Marjorie snippets. But it didn't last long: The New Savoyards, a sort of second-string or feeder to the D'Oyly Carte Opera Company, was coming to the Palace Theatre in Wharton, and Pearl declared herself 'in love' with their leading man and lady, who just happened to be married to one another. They were, she assured me, '*so* in love with each other' that it gave another dimension to the pleasure of watching the performance. 'You can just tell,' she said, nodding vigorously, shaking free a rogue earring and almost bouncing out of her chair, 'you can see the little secret signs they give each other.'

For days we talked of little else. I was already a Gilbert and Sullivan fan, but had never seen a professional performance. Pearl brought in pictures; she had a scrapbook of '*People I Love*', in which she had pasted newspaper clippings of most of the current cast. I noticed the album held no photos of Cyril or Marjorie, though Mother and Simon (including one of the two of them taken with Henry) were well represented. We chewed like a pair of hungry dogs with a bone over which operettas they might perform, listing the various merits and drawbacks of each one, and which we might go to see: Pearl with her mother, of course, and me alone – except for a sort of imaginary man of my dreams, who – unsurprisingly – was a lot like Angus. He was good for my solitary visits to the theatre and concerts. *He* was right beside me instead of playing in the orchestra (my earlier fantasy on such occasions) and made interesting conversation in my head.

I couldn't really afford it, but when they opened the box office I got fairly decent seats for The Yeomen of the Guard on the Tuesday; Iolanthe on the Friday; and, with my mother who was paying for us both, bless her, The Mikado for the Saturday matinee. And as soon as she knew my plans, Pearl booked exactly the same in different parts of the theatre for herself and her mother. This was irritating – if we were going to spy all there was to see going on between Matthew Dexter and Helen Easton, the aforementioned leads, it would have made much better sense to go to different performances. We nearly fell out over it: I said I couldn't understand why on earth she had to go to the same ones I had chosen and she said she knew she'd enjoy them more, just knowing I was in the theatre at the same time.

'That's ridiculous!' I snorted, and put my knitting (a complicated fair isle cardigan that wasn't going too well anyway) into the drawer, which I then slammed shut for good measure.

There were about five minutes of atmospheric silence and then the phone rang: Edna Betty asking Officer Stevens to ask Pearl to ask me to fetch a round sliced milk loaf from Wimbushes.

'Why on earth she can't just ask me straight out...' I harrumphed as I prepared to set off to the bakery. 'She can't think *he* actually goes out and gets it.'

After producing the bread money from her petty cash box, Pearl fished in her handbag and said, proffering some coins, 'Let me treat us to a nice cake each whilst you're there?' and I, recognising it for the olive branch that it clearly was, took the money and said 'thank you, that would be very nice', and harmony was restored.

I was a bit rattled though. Despite the smoothing over of the (albeit, tiny) altercation, the underlying issue still troubled me, and I thought that frankly, I'd have enjoyed myself more if we *hadn't* been in the same space. It wasn't as if Pearl was going to acknowledge my presence there, quite the reverse: she'd pretend to her mother that she didn't even know me. Oh... maybe she got some sort of pleasure from the subterfuge; finding a way to connect with me without her mother knowing. A bit infantile, but then, that was Pearl. I couldn't let it spoil my pleasure in the event.

When I returned with the sliced milk loaf for the Stevens' tea, a chocolate éclair for Pearl and a synthetic cream-filled meringue for myself, she greeted me with great excitement. 'What a shame, Alice, you missed a call from Marjorie!'

A shame indeed, but nothing I could do about it. She'd rung, Pearl said, to make sure Pearl knew about The New Savoyards coming to the Palace. 'As if I wouldn't! But it was terribly kind of her to care, don't you think? She does look out for me, you know.'

'Is she a Gilbert and Sullivan fan, Pearl?' I really *didn't* want to foster yet another discussion of how much Pearl's friends look out for her and how wonderfully they all care about her.

'Oh yes, she's as keen as we are. She and Angus would go every night if they could – they can afford it, of course, the very best seats, probably a box – but Angus has commitments that week, important meetings and things. They're going to the opening night and the closing night though.'

'But that's insane, it's The Mikado both times!' I couldn't hide my surprise.

'That's how much they love Gilbert and Sullivan, Alice.' She made an annoying little gesture with her mouth and tilted her head on one side, losing the other earring in the process. She might just as well have said '*so there!*'; it was explicit in her face.

I couldn't work out why there was so much tension between us over The New Savoyards. I don't think I was any more annoying over them than I had been over anything else, but Pearl seemed suddenly downright prickly about them. Or was she being prickly about Angus and Marjorie, or a combination of the two? I didn't know, but I didn't feel I wanted to spend too much energy on it, so I busied myself with trying to rescue the fair isle cardigan whilst Pearl clattered away, writing to one of her legions of '*lovely, absolutely lovely* friends', all of whom cared and worried desperately about her. Or so she frequently said.

When she went to the toilet about half an hour later I quickly sneaked a look at the letter to see if she'd told her lovely friends what a crabby bitch I was becoming, but all I could find was a comment about how 'my lovely sweet Alice worries about me and looks after me so caringly'. I also noticed – and smirked smugly – that she spelled 'can't' with the apostrophe before the n instead of after it.

Next morning I thought about taking an unspoken conciliatory bunch of freesias to Pearl, but when I saw there was a small queue at the stall, decided, with no little relief, not to bother. All seemed back to normal in the office, though and true to form, it wasn't long before Pearl launched into another tale of Matthew and Helen on stage together, sharing their tremendous love for each other with those who were astute enough – like Pearl, and as she *just knew* I would be – to see it.

'I know Gilbert wrote it that Matthew's roles never end up with the mezzo-soprano, but I think there's a different story there and *he* really wants to. I think Sullivan would have liked that, too. You can just tell that when Matthew is Koko, how he looks at Pitti Sing with such yearning. And the business between them on stage, it's *so* affectionate, so romantic. Though there was one time, last time I saw them, you could just tell they'd had a bit of a tiff, but then they'd obviously made up in the interval and were as sweet as ever together in the second act. Actually, even sweeter. That was Yeomen of the Guard; he was Jack Point and *so* obviously in love with Phoebe. You can tell when he sings the ''hey-de'' song…he's *really* singing to Phoebe.' She sighed dreamily. 'They have a daughter, you know, Matthew and Helen; they've named her Bridget, after Bridget D'Oyly Carte, of course.'

I was hooked. I was slightly, ever so slightly, repelled by Pearl's fantasies about people she really knew very little about, but in reality it was only what I had spent my childhood doing and secretly still did occasionally (and resolved to do less of from now on). So I encouraged her, and from time to time we would hypothesise possible scenarios and ways of being for Matthew Dexter and Helen Easton.

EIGHT

And so began The Game. It started simply and innocently enough: we slipped seamlessly after a few days from 'I'll bet Matthew says...', or 'And then Helen would say....', to becoming the voice for one or the other. I don't remember which of us made the jump first, but obviously the other was happy to go along with the improvement. To begin with either of us would 'be' either of them, but as The Game continued we seemed to settle on Pearl taking the male role as I took the female even when we included other characters in our little dramas. Sometimes we would be Marjorie and Angus. In fact, it actually started with them in the sense that we'd frequently do the 'I'll bet Angus says...' bit, but that version never really took off for us. Possibly because we somehow felt we'd only be able to use things we already knew, rather than inventing scenes for them; they were more known quantities. Or maybe it just felt a bit too close to the bone for Pearl, for whom they were – presumably – well-known, real-life people. At any rate, we gradually dropped them (without any conversation or consultation about it) and spent hours each day playing The Helen and Matthew Game – which we never actually referred to or called anything. We'd just slide into it, with either of us voicing the first line. I don't think I called it anything to myself, either. If I thought about it at all, I thought of it in terms of 'doing it', and looked forward to more of the same.

Each scenario was different: we 'did' their first meeting, the first time he asked her out, their first going out together followed by many, many variations of the same episode, progressing their relationship. We did him asking her to marry him and her reluctance and shyness, and constant conferring with other members of the company, all of whom looked out for her and took wonderfully loving care of her and her great emotional vulnerability. We did her discovering she was pregnant and how she told him, and what his overjoyed reaction was; we even did the baby's birth (as always, all words, no physical stuff at all!) I, as Helen, was wonderfully brave and hardly screamed at all. Pearl, as Matthew was moved to tears by my incredible courage, and she actually managed to produce real tears. And when we'd worked

46

through all that, we created misunderstandings, rows, near-estrangements and of course their ultimate tender resolutions.

They may have been different episodes, yet each scene was very much the same in the sense that an amazing amount of rescuing, understanding, forgiving, and emotional care and attention went into every one. Those were the best bits for me, giving me the eagerly anticipated frissons and making me want more, more, more. I pushed to move us more into that type of interaction; Pearl's apparent preference was for more of the slushy, loving talk.

And in between there were odd bits of work from Officer Stevens, several 'He's gone again!' episodes from Officer Park, and a never-ending onslaught of cheerfully rendered 'all well?' greetings from Officer Hampton. After a lengthy spell of worrying and feeling ill, handyman Morris was diagnosed with a stomach ulcer and took long-term sick leave (Officer Park was detailed to take on the immediate needs of the handyman's job, which didn't go down too well with him; he thought he'd been selected because he was 'common', and I suspect he was right) and I abandoned my fair isle cardigan in favour of an easier, more subtle striped jumper. Angus and Marjorie stories continued spasmodically, as did Marjorie's lunchtime phone calls. Her opening gambit was always the same: 'How *is* my dear Pearl?', usually followed by a variation on the theme of 'We do worry about her, she's *so* incredibly brave' and 'She is *so* grateful to you, Alice, for looking after her so tenderly'. At first my guilt prompted me to try harder to 'look after her tenderly' (whatever that meant), but it never seemed to last very long.

Nor, usually, could I bring myself to tell Pearl that Marjorie had phoned. It would only lead to a stomach-churning (mine) monologue (Pearl's) on how *lovely* the whole Browne (with an e) family was and how much they cared for Pearl and how they all worried so much about her and her health. And anyway, since the whole point of Marjorie's calls seemed to be aimed at finding out if the courageous Pearl was still putting one foot in front of the other – which she was – there didn't seem to be much point in mentioning it, and I *really* didn't want to feed her annoying obsession with how all her lovely friends worried and cared so much about her. I never got any titbits of useful information from Marjorie, who always seemed to ring from a phone box, though I never asked why.

The problem was, I didn't really like Pearl. Her obsession with herself and her health bothered me, and I found her too effusive about me, about music, about God, about just about everything. Practically every other sentence she uttered was filled with italics and ended with an exclamation mark, so summoning the energy to respond appropriately was frankly exhausting at times. I often felt like telling her that my English teacher had taught that we each are issued with two exclamation marks at birth, and when we've used them, that's it – there aren't any more. Pearl was so far into the red with her usage that such a revelation from me could only have caused an atmosphere between us.

We began having silly arguments. For example, me, stupidly: 'That woman in the music shop reminds me of Helen Easton.'

'Oh, Alice, she isn't anything *like* Helen.' Her, exasperated and smiling smugly and fiddling with either her too-big ring or her refusing-to-stay-put earrings. Or both.

'No, I didn't say she was *like* her, I said she *reminds* me of Helen. You know, puts me in mind of... not looks like,' snottily.

'You're just being silly, Alice, she's nothing like her,' condescendingly.

'Well, she still makes me think of her and there's not much you can do about that,' triumphantly. Then there would be long silences between us until one of us found something innocuous to comment on – more often than not the '*all well*?' arrival of Officer Hampton; he was good for that – and harmony was restored.

We were in reasonably harmonious form when Pearl's mother took another trip to North Wales, so when Pearl invited me to go to a concert with her in Birmingham – her treat – and then home to spend the night with her, I accepted happily enough.

We took the bus to Birmingham after work and had beans on toast in a seedy little café down a side street from Symphony Hall, where Pearl pointed out various couples, analysing the state of their relationships based on what she could see. 'They've just had a row, probably over the children, but they'll make up tonight,' and 'Those two should never have got married, but they haven't the courage to do the decent thing and end it now, whilst they still have a chance for lasting happiness'. And it didn't stop when we moved into the concert hall and settled into our seats. Then she gushed over the first violin when he appeared and almost swooned at the sight of the handsome young conductor. When the music began, she listened annoyingly; her tiny little squeaks of pleasure kept interrupting my concentration and I felt I had to practically sit on my hands to stop her grabbing and squeezing them. I tried to join in her enthusiasm for the '*beautiful*' conductor, and idiotically suggested we might write to him and tell him how much we had enjoyed his interpretation of the Dances of Galanta. (I was at that annoying stage of mouthing platitudes like 'I don't know much about music, but I know what I like' – and I *really* liked the Dances of Galanta.)

Pearl was thrilled by the idea, so we spent the bus journey back to her house crafting the (frankly sickeningly sycophantic) letter, to be sent next day. We even asked for a signed photograph. We argued a little over the spelling of memento; Pearl was convinced it was spelled 'momento', 'No, Alice, it's *mo*mento. You know, it's something *momentous,* a memory of the *moment*, that's what we're asking for.'

'I'm sure you're right, Pearl,' I was already learning not to labour any points, and decided to do it my way anyway, and just not tell her. After all, I reasoned, what could I expect from a person who can't spell 'can't' correctly. So, walking past the only anywhere-near-posh shop at this end of Westfield, I distracted her by pointing out the two gorgeous diaphanous nighties in their display window. 'Look at those, Pearl, they are just the kind of nighties Matthew would want Helen to wear, but she'd be too shy.'

It worked. 'So Matthew would buy them for her and one evening, when he felt the time was right, he'd undress her in

49

front of the fire and put one of them on her.' She grabbed my arm and tucked her hand practically into my armpit. 'Oh I do so love spending time with you, Alice, we are so *compatible,*' she enthused, lolling her head on my shoulder. 'Now, I haven't made up Simon's bed, you're going to share with me, and that's that. I'm not taking no for an answer. I can't have you being cold all night again.'

I took as long as I could in the bathroom to make sure Pearl was safely ensconced first. I prayed she wouldn't want us to 'do' Matthew and Helen with the damn chiffon nighties, or worse, to re-enact the McIntoshes' first night. I didn't fancy being undressed by Pearl, romantic though the Angus and Marjorie scene had felt when we'd talked about it and included it in our strictly talking-only Game (it had been a good one). But just to be on the safe side, I kept my bra and knickers on under my serviceable and utterly non-sexy pyjamas.

I slid into the bed and hunched myself on the extreme edge, but it was no use. 'Oh dear, the bed's so cold, let's cuddle up and get warm,' she whispered. I pretended not to hear, but she said it again, so I shifted about an inch and a half towards the middle. She was already there, scrawny arms outstretched and ready to envelop me.

Staying as still as I could, hoping I'd just fall asleep, I felt sick. I stuck it as long as I could – probably no more than three or four minutes – and then pulled away. 'I'm *too* hot now, Pearl, so I'll stay on the side if you don't mind. I'm not used to sleeping with someone else.' What a hypocrite I was – I'd have given my back teeth to sleep all night cuddled up to Jack in our getting-on days.

'Oh that's all right dear. I just want you to be comfy, darling Alice. And in any case, it's so lovely just to have you here to talk to, and it will be heaven to wake up with you here tomorrow morning.'

Somehow I got through the night. I didn't sleep much, wondering what on earth I was playing at. What was I doing in this bed with this woman? Most distressing of all was the question of whom I could talk to about what was going on. It was easy to think Pearl was crackers, twisted by thwarted love, but what about me? How could I play these weird semi-erotic games in broad daylight in the office, but then be so standoffish in the present situation.

Well, the truth was, I was repelled by Pearl, I suppose. Playing The Game was different, I reasoned; Pearl wasn't Pearl then, any more than I was Alice. We *became* Matthew and Helen. At least *I* became Helen. I don't really know what went on for Pearl because we never, ever talked about it. Becoming someone else had been a near constant behaviour for me for as far back as I could remember, until I connected with Jack when suddenly it seemed preferable to be me, Alice Chorley, and I gave it a break. Pearl was a useful addition to something I'd done for as long as I could remember, but I was also quite content to continue the fantasies on my own, outside office hours.

I don't think I ever felt I wanted to talk to Pearl about what was happening. I did, occasionally, wonder at the circumstances that had landed me in the company of someone who would apparently willingly do what I had spent a lifetime doing, mostly by myself, and often feeling there must be something *really* wrong with me because of it. I still felt that, but over the years had got better and better at batting away those thoughts. Except in the small hours of a dark night, sharing a bed with Pearl.

NINE

The New Savoyards' week in Wharton provided plenty of fodder for The Game. Each day the Wharton paper wrote generously about them, reviewing the previous night's offering in glowing terms and often adding a small 'human interest' story that we happily, greedily, used wherever possible to add to our repertoire. We learned, for example, that Helen Easton's family lived in Southsea and, from the article, it seemed that Helen spent most of her free time there. There was no reference to a child, and what Matthew did in any free time wasn't mentioned; in fact you wouldn't know they were married from the newspaper reports. I said as much, to Pearl, knowing I was being provocative and actually, perversely, taking some pleasure in it.

'But they are,' affirmed Pearl, emphasising this with her annoying head-nodding and pursed lips, another habit I had added to the rapidly growing list of things about her I couldn't stand, along with the ever-dangling earrings that were forever dropping off. Why on earth didn't she get her ears pierced instead of persisting with these old-fashioned screw-back efforts?

This detail on Helen and Matthew's relationship, or, more accurately, lack of detail, provided us with another strand to our Game: we decided their relationship was 'struggling', so a lot of our acted-out stories involved misunderstandings, accusations, retribution and, best of all, reconciliations. And of course, Matthew was never anything but totally loving and understanding, willing – apparently – to put up with just about any emotional abuse from his over-sensitive wife. In fact, an awful lot like Angus, according to Pearl

Work obligations – such as they were – weekends, and Officer Park and his runaway son frankly got in our way. And in the very week of The New Savoyards' visit, Chief Officer Stevens decided to make a bigger-than-usual effort with his quarterly position paper. Poor old Pearl was kept busy typing and retyping, making it impossible for us to play The Game. I had much less to do, so kept myself occupied with knitting my stripy jumper, making extra cups of tea for Pearl, and running future Game scenes in my head. Eventually Officer Stevens was satisfied and it was completed, but not before we had run off (on the hand-cranked copying machine) and collated seventeen copies of twenty-five pages each. That was fairly mindless work: I ran off the required copies of each page as it was completed and we then laid it all out on the conference room table, so all we had to do was walk around collecting a page from each pile and staple the lot together. It took us longer than it should have, partly because we spent so much time chatting, and partly because, to be honest, we weren't used to actually working. But it was a nice opportunity to bring Pearl up to date with my latest imaginings, all of which were received by her with approval and an occasional addition, which I was careful not to reject. I didn't mind arguing with Pearl about most things, but not about scenes for The Game. Somehow that was sacred. Possibly she felt the same, though of course we never talked about that either.

We also discussed to a nearly mind-numbing depth the operetta we had seen the night before or the night before that, and all we had imagined going on between Matthew and Helen. There probably *wasn't* anything going on, but that didn't stop us, so having seen all three officers safely off to the main Council Offices with their precious plan, we set about acting out our latest scenes. Pearl repeatedly proclaimed herself thrilled with my new offerings, and launched herself in with gusto, even adding a few new touches of her own.

And all this, as always, was accomplished with absolutely no physical touching on our part, ever. I think we did once spread a blanket out on the floor when we were 'having a picnic together' as Helen and Matthew, but as I recall, we never actually sat on it. Our Game would not have made good television – it was ideal for the radio though.

It's hard to describe the sensation I felt when we were doing The Game. It wasn't a sexual feeling. At least not in the same way my sofa sex sessions with Jack had been. It was a tingly feeling, centred in my upper belly, a feeling that my school friend Pat and I had called a frisson, and which arose when one or other of the objects of our schoolgirl crushes had looked at us, or made some personal remark. It would never, could never, have led to an orgasm; it was totally unconnected to my genitals. But it was addictive, all the same. It's what kept me coming back for more of the same with Pearl, and spurred me on to learn more and more about the key players in our drama, the better to act out our frisson-making moments.

We really knew very little about them, Helen and Matthew. The sum total of our actual knowledge would not have made for much of a Game, actually: they were both leads in The New Savoyards; they were or had been married to one another; Helen lived (mostly) with her family in Southsea. I don't know where Pearl got the information that they had a child ('I just *know* it, Alice. Why can't you just accept that?') so that may or may not have been a reality. In fact, I'm not sure where she learned they were married to each other; that could have been her invention or wishful thinking, too. Though it obviously didn't matter in Game terms.

Even though I'd become used to going to concerts and the theatre by myself, it felt really strange that even though we were going to the same theatre to see the same performance, it was all done quite separately. If the shoe had been on the other foot, I know I would have taken Pearl home to tea with me and then the three of us (me, Pearl, Mother) would have made our way to Wharton in plenty of time for curtain-up. I said nothing to Pearl about this, partly because I was used to it and in any case knew what she'd say in response, but also because I don't think I really wanted to spend any time outside the office with her, and certainly not with Mother. I knew where they were sitting – in the stalls; I was in the balcony – so it wasn't hard to avoid them, and I kept telling myself how glad I was *not* to be sitting next to the hand-grabbing, squeaking-with-pleasure Pearl – and the notoriously cantankerous Mother (who'd actually only ever been perfectly polite and nice to me on the few occasions she'd come in to our office).

My mother was a different story, however. She simply did not understand why we weren't allowed to make contact with Pearl and her mother. 'Can't we even *wave?*' So I told her, again, what Pearl had said: that Mother was so jealous of Pearl's friends that she made the poor woman's life a misery with her criticism so, for Pearl, simply not having any friends of her own was the obvious solution. This made for a difficult afternoon for me at the matinee performance of The Mikado. I found it hard to concentrate on the stage – and any little nuances between Helen and Matthew – because I couldn't help being aware of my mother simmering away in what was, in reality, perfectly justified anger at the Taylor women's behaviour. Her solution was that I should not be 'so nice' to Pearl, and obviously didn't believe me when I said 'I'm *not*, I'm not nice to or about her, at all.'

'Hmm…' she grunted, which for her was never the end of a conversation; merely a pause whilst she marshalled her mental forces, ready for another attack. I sighed, and decided we'd have to go straight home after the show rather than linger in the nice little pub opposite the theatre as we'd planned.

Pearl, the two mothers, Matthew and Helen aside, I was completely taken with professionally presented Gilbert and Sullivan and felt I couldn't wait two years or more before they came again to our area. My whole family had been members of an amateur dramatic and music society all my life, and over the years we had put on a number of G&S operas, so I was quite familiar with many of the stories. (I'd only ever had brief walk-on parts or behind the scenes chores suitable for a child to get involved with.) During the week of their visit, Pearl, a regular reader of *The Stage*, had almost accidentally discovered in it The New Savoyards' schedule for the rest of the year. Their last stop on this current tour, in September, was Southsea: 'They'll be staying with her parents, you can be sure of that,' stated Pearl. 'Then they'll stay there for the winter and be a proper family with little Bridget.'

Cramming down my irritation at the sickly epithet '*little*' Bridget, I decided on the spot that I, too, would go to Southsea. I'd take Friday as a holiday to travel, get a cheap and cheerful B&B on the sea front, buy an inexpensive ticket for the Saturday matinee, and come home on Sunday afternoon – after having a prowl round the posh streets of Southsea. I thought if I looked in the phone book I might find out where exactly the Eastons lived.

If Pearl had come up with this plan for herself (not a chance, not with Mother permanently glued to her side) I would have been horribly jealous; but if Pearl was, she didn't show it, at least not then. She was most encouraging and even went to the library one lunchtime (thus angering Mother, she told me in great detail, who expected her home at one fifteen '*on the dot!*') to look in their countrywide collection of telephone directories for the Easton's address. She found two in Southsea, she reported, but no indication of anything other than the address and the listed person's initial.

'I also looked up Dexter, M, but there weren't any. In any case, I made sure he and Helen would be ex-directory anyway.'

'Made sure' was one of Pearl's speech idiosyncrasies that threatened to drive me crackers. What she meant was 'I was sure'. From time to time I'd ask archly *how* she'd 'made sure' exactly, and she'd look chagrined and say, 'Oh Alice, you know what I mean, I *was* sure', and I'd feel half triumphant and half a bitchy cow. She never made any attempt to change it though, and I think that annoyed me more than anything. Maybe she thought it was endearing, along with bravado, which she pronounced brave-aydoh. And who knows, maybe to Cyril they had been.

I was a groupie – a stalker – long before the term had been invented. Fortunately I didn't know this. If I thought about it at all, I suppose I thought I was quite resourceful and should be admired. Pearl, who was as big a groupie as anyone, had actually been the one to suggest 'a casual walk by' the Easton residence, but it gave me what I thought was a brilliant – but never to be disclosed to Pearl – idea: I looked in the Westfield telephone directory in our office and found the Brownes (with an e – there was only one of them) on Garden Road, which easily qualified as the posh area Pearl had said they lived in. And the following lunchtime, I set off to see what sort of house Cyril and his family lived in. Assuming it was them and that they weren't also ex-directory. You never know with posh people.

I had no idea what I thought I might see, or what I might learn from such an expedition, and not surprisingly, I discovered nothing at all worth noting. It was a large house – they all were in that area – set well back from the road, so not very visible. There were no cars in their drive and no sign of any life anywhere on the property. There seemed to be a huge lawn behind the house, and the bit at the front, nearest the road, was crammed with ghastly green (low-maintenance) bushes. I couldn't see any flowers or a colour other than green anywhere. All in all it was a great disappointment and not at all what I would have wanted for *my* prospective in-laws.

But it led to another thought: where might Angus and Marjorie live, and, come to that, where in Wharton did Angus practise? Before Pearl's little library expedition, I hadn't thought of telephone books, but a trip to the library next day during lunch to look at their Yellow Pages and the Wharton telephone directory revealed no Angus McIntosh, Doctor of Dentistry, and, not so unexpectedly perhaps, no McIntoshes listed in and around Wharton. That wasn't so surprising, they were probably ex-directory as so many professional people were, but why wasn't he listed in the Yellow Pages as a dentist? He was, naturally, a private dentist, so wouldn't he need to advertise? How on earth did his patients contact him if he didn't have an easy-to-find telephone number? Pat's conviction of their non-existence seemed more and more plausible.

TEN

'I've got some lovely titbits for you, Alice,' Pearl greeted me on the Monday after our frankly emotionally draining Gilbert and Sullivan week.

'Oh yes?' I was already feeling flat now that the intensity of the past week was over, so felt very ready to hear something stimulating from Pearl.

'Marjorie and Angus are great friends of the manager of the Palace of course, so on Saturday morning when Marjorie was in town she dropped into the theatre to have coffee with him, and who do you suppose walked into his office?'

I knew she wanted me to guess and get it wrong so, not really in a mood to be too obliging, I simply shrugged my shoulders and raised my eyebrows. But I smiled encouragingly.

'Matthew and Helen! That's who!'

'Wow!' I was impressed and thrilled, and sat back to listen as Pearl told me they'd been introduced to Marjorie. They had apparently stayed only briefly, but long enough for Matthew to point out that Helen, who'd helped herself to one of the manager's hot buttered crumpets, had dripped some butter down her chin.

'They were so lovely with one another, Marjorie said. She said he reached over and so tenderly wiped her mouth and chin with his lovely white linen hankie and said "You've got butter all over your face. You're all greasy, little Miss Muffet." And when he went – before Helen left – he said something in Russian. Marjorie wrote it down for me, it was *"Dosvidanya moya bezkouetchno krasivaya."*

'I wonder what it means.'

'Oh Marjorie knew, she speaks Russian, you know. It means *"goodbye my most beautiful one".*'

'Oh, that *is* lovely. How romantic. Oh lucky, lucky Marjorie. What were they wearing – did she say?'

Pearl looked up at the ceiling thoughtfully. 'Yes, she did. He was wearing dark brown wide wale corduroys and a mustard yellow jumper. And Helen had a matching yellow jumper and beige linen slacks. She said they both looked very arty, wearing sandals, and Matthew was smoking a pipe; just as you'd expect theatre folk to look on a Saturday morning, she said.'

'Yes, nice,' I approved of the outfits and the pipe. 'Anything else?'

'No, I've told you, they only stayed a very short while. I expect they had things to do in the theatre before the matinee.'

'The performance *we* saw! I wish we'd known she might have butter on her chin, Little Miss Muffet,' I sighed.

'Don't be silly, Alice. Make Up would have taken care of it anyway, even if Matthew hadn't.'

We chewed over our new information for the rest of the morning, both of us obviously imagining how we could work it into The Game. It was acting out gold for us. We were both good at creating stories and story lines, but a bit of help from the outside never hurt. And 'Little Miss Muffet': what a charming epithet!

My friend Pat, who worked in her boyfriend's company office in Westfield, came over at lunchtime, bringing the usual fabulous hot dogs with fried onions from the market. She was a satisfying – and outraged – audience for the saga of Pearl and her mother's 'don't come near us' injunctions, and as intrigued as I was with the news of Marjorie's visit to the theatre manager, although she knew nothing about The Game, of course. Her interest was because she was convinced that Pearl was making the whole thing up, from Cyril to Marjorie and Angus, and everything in between. And not for the first time said so.

'No, she can't be – Marjorie has rung here several times and I've spoken to her,' I still really wanted to believe in it all, it was so romantic as well as just plain interesting.

'And never when Pearl is here. Right?' Silence. Then, 'Does she sound like Pearl?'

'*NO*! Well... a little bit, I suppose. But they are both Westfield born and raised, so that's not surprising. Marjorie sounds posher than Pearl though.'

'Hmm,' Pat finished her second hot dog and licked her lips. 'When did our Marge pass this information onto Pearl? She told you on Monday that it had happened on Saturday morning; you lot went on Saturday afternoon and they went to the performance on Saturday night didn't they? So she must have told Pearl on Sunday then. Unless they passed in the street between performances, which is not too likely.'

'Oh gosh, yes, you must be right. Marjorie couldn't have phoned Pearl because she isn't on the phone. And she does things with her mother every Sunday... though I suppose she could have gone out and phoned Marjorie... Yes, I'll bet that's what happened. Pearl rang her on Sunday to find out how she'd enjoyed the Mikado.'

'Then how did Marge write down the Russian bit for Pearl?'

'Jesus! *I* don't know, Pat. Maybe Pearl gave her mother the slip and met Marjorie for afternoon tea – or they go to the same church or something. Don't *look* at me like that!' Pat's eyebrows were nearly out of sight under her hairline. 'Or maybe Marjorie didn't actually write it down but spelled it out for Pearl to write down. Don't make something out of nothing all the time.' I began angrily clearing away the debris from our lunch. I was all the more irritated because I knew Pat's questions were perfectly reasonable. She was only giving voice to thoughts I wasn't allowing myself to have. I didn't want to have them; I wasn't ready to.

'Where do they live?' Pat was not going to be silenced. 'I think we ought to have a mooch round one Saturday afternoon and maybe even pay them a visit. You know, "we're a bit lost and wondered if we could use your phone'' sort of thing.'

'Good idea. Except I don't *know* where they live.'

'Where they're supposed to live, you mean. Well, ask the lovely Pearl and let me know. And next time Marge rings, ask her to say something in Russian.'

Pat had just left to go back to her office when Marjorie did ring, but of course I didn't confront her. I did ask her how she'd enjoyed the Mikado and hoped she'd tell me about seeing Matthew and Helen in the theatre manager's office, but she didn't take the bait. She went straight into her obsessive concern about Pearl's health, which always seemed perfectly fine to me – at least physically; I wasn't so sure about her mental state – but then I hadn't known her when she'd almost died over the loss of Cyril.

For the first time since I'd started work in this office, I longed for the day to be over so I could get on my bus and consider the various aspects in peace. I didn't really want to play The Game today, so made up my mind not to respond to any attempt by Pearl to get it started but to my relief she didn't try. I didn't tell her that Marjorie had rung and she, for some reason she didn't explain, wasn't very communicative with me either, spending the afternoon writing to one or more of her hordes of caring friends. I knew I was supposed to ask her what was wrong, but I couldn't find the energy this time, so began a letter of my own to a cousin I hadn't seen for years. We thus spent the afternoon in not what you'd call 'companionable silence', so I was quite relieved when Edna Betty rang to ask Officer Stevens to ask Pearl to ask me to fetch him a loaf. Which she did, in a monotone and with no other comment.

On my way to the bakery, happy to be out in the fresh air and away from the office atmosphere, I bumped into Pat, who was on her way to the post office.

'Guess what?' She grabbed my arm as I attempted to hurry to Wimbushes before they ran out of the only bread the Stevens family apparently ever ate.

'I don't know. What?'

'You'll never guess who I saw in the phone box by the bus station on my way back to my office at lunchtime. Actually, I'll bet you *will* guess…'

'Pearl?' For some reason I whispered it.

'Yep, the old fake Pearl herself. I'd recognise that draggy-hem skirt poking out under her coat a mile away.'

'Did she see you?'

'I think she did; she must have cos she turned away so her back was towards the street. I don't think she'd have done that if she hadn't spotted me.' She smiled provocatively, head on one side, 'So tell me, did Marge ring today, right after I left?'

'Well, you know, Pearl doesn't *have* a phone at home, so she might have wanted to talk to someone with me hearing.' I don't know why I felt so annoyed with Pat, nor why I didn't answer her direct question. I wanted to go on believing, I suppose. If the phone calls from Marjorie were in reality Pearl pretending to her, what sort of a fool was I? 'Anyway, gotta run, there'll be hell to pay if I don't round up a blasted sliced round milk loaf for the boss.' And off I went, brain spinning like an out-of-control windmill, and knowing full well I was not going to confront Pearl with this latest piece of possibly incriminating information. I wasn't sure who I despised more as I realised that: Pearl or me.

ELEVEN

The mood in the office stayed a bit sombre for several days, so eventually I decided I couldn't take it any longer and would confront it. That morning I'd had a response from the lovely conductor we'd written to, but if Pearl was going to be in this mood, I didn't think I wanted to share it. Resolutely telling myself I was ready for anything, I asked Pearl if she was all right. After first saying 'Oh yes,' quite coldly, she said 'Sorry, I know I've gone a bit quiet, dear Alice, but I'm struggling to deal with things inside at the moment.'

Biting back the almost overwhelming urge to say 'why on earth didn't you *tell* me, Pearl?' I said 'Oh gosh, Pearl, poor you. If there's anything I can do to help...' I began to feel guilty over my uncharitable thoughts about her lately, but also dreaded what might be coming. Surely not some other hapless male desperately in love with her and wanting her hand in marriage. Oh no, please not that again.

'You are such a love, Alice, but no. It's just memories... my friend Ellen – you know, who went to Australia – my lovely, lovely Ellen... reminded me in her last letter of the present Cyril sent her for Christmas that year. She was the only person to get a present from him that year because he... because his accident... because... well, he wasn't here...' She looked dangerously close to tears, which I definitely didn't want, guilt or no guilt. 'It hurts me here,' she continued, pressing her scraggy hands to her somewhat flattened bosom.

I recognised the phrase, having just read it in *Pilgrim Cottage,* but also knew that I was often guilty of lifting useful phrases for future appropriate use. After all, when I'd backed off the idea of marrying and Jack had said 'but you were so sure, Spud,' hadn't I responded with the line I'd squirrelled away from The Admirable Crichton, which we had just seen together: '*I'll never be sure of anything again.*'

'What did he send her?' Maybe that would stop her getting too maudlin.

'Oh Alice, he sent her a *beautiful* leather-bound very rare first edition of the Palgrave *Golden Treasury*. That's why it

63

was the only thing I could give you for your birthday – although obviously not a rare first edition.' She smiled weakly.

'Oh.' What else could I say? *Why* was it the only thing she could give me for my birthday? How was her relationship with me in any way like her about-to-be fiancé's relationship with her best friend? Sometimes I felt I could read Pearl like an open book, but at other times, like now, I was completely confused by her peculiar thinking and nonsensical logic.

'Do you know what he wrote in it, Alice?'

I shook my head. How the hell could I know? Except it would be something soppy, I felt sure of that.

'He wrote "To the dear one of my dear one". Wasn't that lovely? He'd never met Ellen of course, but he *knew* how important to me she was and how desperately I missed her.'

I did my by now much-practised empathetic nod and grunt, and waited what I hoped was a discreet interval before saying, 'I think I've got something that will raise your spirits'.

Pearl sniffed bravely and looked at me sorrowfully as I waved the photograph of the unrealistically handsome Paul Mullins, associate conductor of the City of Birmingham Symphony Orchestra, at her. She cheered up instantly.

'Oh, he's *so* gorgeous. Oh thank you, Alice, you've made my day and completely taken away my despondent mood. What a treasure you are, what would I ever do without you?'

I shrugged. It was hard even for me to believe I had that much power over a person's mood, especially *improving* it. And even harder to believe in her abject misery changing quite so rapidly to this rampant enthusiasm.

'Was there a letter with it, or just the photograph? Oh he's so good-looking...'

I showed her the letter. I wasn't an expert in responses to fan mail, but it did seem to me that he'd written – in purple ink and rather flamboyantly large handwriting – a pretty decent response to our effusive appreciation of his rendering of the Dances of Galanta. *'I'm pleased you found it so exciting; it's a notoriously difficult piece to conduct appropriately,'* he'd written, along with '*my thanks for bothering to write'.*

'I wonder if he's married,' Pearl sat looking rapt at the photograph. Oh, here we go, I thought, and sure enough, 'I've noticed a very distinguished-looking lady in the stalls when he's conducting and she's always by herself.'

And off we went. By going-home time we'd given him three children (at three different posh boarding schools), 'difficulties' with his wife that they were working hard to resolve, a mansion in Warwickshire, and his just-about-managed addiction to gambling.

'Which is why he never gets beyond associate conductor,' declared Pearl. 'The management don't feel able to trust him. And he *isn't* trustworthy if he doesn't have a good woman behind him. But he knew that, that's why he's finally confessed to her. And she's faithful; you can tell that, the way she sits in the audience night after night, leading the applause. Always in that seat so he knows just where she is and can snatch a quick look at her for support. *She* wants it to work out, but he's not so sure. You see, gambling is his first love.'

Swallowing my somewhat reluctant admiration for Pearl's swift and on-the-spot creation of a whole lifestyle for this unknown conductor, I joined in. 'I think he might be secretly in love with the woman who sits next to the leader of the second violins.' As I got into it, I was actually quite happy to embellish this episode of The Game, with Paul Mullins now starring. There wasn't much going on with Matthew and Helen, or with Angus and Marjorie these days – we'd run out of steam, so we might as well incorporate Paul and Athena (the name we'd given her because, Pearl said, she looked Greek) into The Game.

'But she isn't sure about him, the violinist. She's interested, but because of her past, she's too afraid of getting hurt. I mean, he *is* married and he obviously *wants* to make a go of it with Athena.'

'Is Athena secretly attracted to someone else too?' I thought we might add yet another dimension.

'Oh no, she's entirely faithful, but because of her background she's... oh no, wait, *he's* a bit stand-offish and slow to warm up in bed. Athena's passionate and hot-blooded, being Greek, but very understanding of his restricted emotions, of course. Well, she tries to be, but it's hard... it's not what she expected when she married him.'

'It's a duty thing then...'

'...and the management wouldn't like a scandal, not even a separation never mind a divorce.'

And so it went on, growing, shifting, getting itself ready to be acted out with dialogue, perhaps tomorrow. A highly satisfying day at the office.

I hadn't replaced Jack, and I definitely wanted to, but in the meantime I was having a lovely time with all these invented fantasy men. And I now had a much better idea of what sort of man I would be happy with. He had to have a good sense of humour, he had to be kind, he had to be handsome, intelligent, educated, in a professional job, fairly posh, and always perfectly understanding. In other words, pretty much a complete replica of Angus McIntosh. (Though he didn't absolutely have to be Scottish – or a dentist; he could be a doctor, though. Possibly even a vicar? Maybe.) I had no idea where I was ever going to meet this paragon of perfection, of course, but in the meantime the mental image of him (I'd temporarily named him Bruce though god knows why) accompanied me everywhere I went, including bed. And in moments of utter desperation I assured God that I, like Marjorie, would happily wait till my mid-to-late-thirties if I could be assured of ending up with a husband as perfectly marvellous as hers.

TWELVE

'How are you enjoying *Pilgrim Cottage*, Alice?' It was morning coffee time so of course no work would be done. Not that we did much at any other time really, but certainly having a steaming cup of something on the desk meant we definitely downed our tools and chatted.

'Er, yes, it's good, very good, but... well, sometimes it's a bit on the far-fetched side. Too many happy coincidences really; it doesn't quite ring true, don't you think?'

'I know what you mean. You can tell it's written by a man, I always know when it's a man writing; that's a very male fantasy of beautiful rich women falling in love with the young hero, or ugly elderly rich women with hearts of gold wanting to look after him.' Pearl leaned back in her chair, settling in for a deep and meaningful chat about the book.

I thought how the story of Marge-n-Ange (as Pat was now referring to them) was more fantasy-like than real, but didn't say anything. Instead, I wondered how I could find out if the *Pilgrim Cottage* author really was a man, or just a Pearl-like fantasist woman writer using a man's name. It would have given me great (and nasty) satisfaction to spring that on Pearl. I didn't bother to wonder why that was.

Actually, what troubled me more about the book was its rather sickening sentimentality. I could see why Pearl loved it so – the main characters all talked like her (no wonder it was so easy for her to pick up their phrases) – and I desperately hoped I wasn't that soppy. Every character was two-dimensional: totally black and white, all good or all bad. Occasionally, *very* occasionally, a bad character would do something Really Good in a classic triumph of good over evil, but it never rang true, and a good character never ever did anything remotely bad; unless it was to show a bit of a temper, but never too much, of course, and always in a good cause. I was also quite put off by the many chapters on the heroine's sojourn in Russia. The whole premise of her going there under those circumstances was totally unbelievable and the propaganda was so boring that I very nearly gave up. In fact, I was just about to when I came to a bit about the handsome young and idealistic Russian doctor (who'd fallen in love with the English heroine, of course) saying goodbye to her. And he said, *'Dosvidanya moya bezkouetchno krasivaya'*, which was obligingly translated in the text as 'Goodbye my most beautiful one', just as Marjorie had said. Or at least, just as Pearl had said Marjorie had said.

This seemed far more significant to me than her use of 'it hurts me here'; this was a direct steal, plagiarism of a sort, and assigned to our heroes as reported on by a woman my friend Pat was sure did not exist. My brain ached as I thought about this, wondering where the discrepancy lay. I said nothing to Pearl, but I changed my mind about abandoning the book. If nothing else, the protagonists of the first section, Philip and Ann, would do for The Game if we ever ran out of fuel from Matthew and Helen, or Marjorie and Angus. But they'd have to be a lot less sappy than in the book. I'd see to that. And meanwhile, who knew what else I might come across that Pearl had appropriated. I could hardly wait to get home and plough on through the turgid prose.

The Paul and Athena Mullins story never made it onto the stage. We returned to it from time to time in an abstract, discussional way, but never got round to acting it out. Part of the reason was the shift in who was playing which role. I didn't want to play the man (though never said so); my forte was playing the shy, reluctant lover and Pearl's Game-acting strength lay in being the all-understanding, but desperately in love husband. Somehow we had reversed the roles in this pair and it didn't feel right. I didn't want to be the reassurer, I wanted to be reassured. And I didn't want to play the male role, no matter what the issue was or wasn't.

But it didn't matter; we suddenly had other fish to fry. Marjorie, Pearl announced with more than usually irritating fanfare and her characteristic little squeaks of joy, was pregnant, and everybody was overjoyed. Pearl and I were so thrilled in fact that even my ever-present simmering irritation with Pearl vanished immediately; and better yet, Officer Park's 'He's gone again!' son didn't even come close to dampening our happiness.

'You need to tell the police, and prompto,' Pearl stated firmly, mindlessly tossing in another of her misspeaks, 'it's pretty obvious you and your wife can't handle this boy.'

Stunned, Officer Park stood immobile for several seconds, then turned on his heel and stamped out of our office, not quite slamming the door to the glass corridor. Officer Hampton chose that very moment to arrive through the front door, trilling 'All well?' as usual on his way by our corridor.

'No, it bloody isn't!' hissed Park.

'Oh I say, old chap...' chirruped Officer Hampton, and the two of them disappeared into the conference room to have a soothing man-to-man chat over a cup of tea whilst we struggled to regain our equilibrium.

We recovered fairly quickly – 'Gone-Again' was frankly no longer very interesting – and continued our speculation about the McIntosh baby, would it be – did they want – a boy or a girl? What if they had twins? When is it due? What might they name it? Pearl was pretty sure Angus would have a long line of family names that would have to be incorporated. But what might they be? Well Angus would certainly be in there... if it's a boy... and on and on and on.

'Where will she have the baby, Pearl? At home?'

'Oh no, her doctor thinks because of her age she might have trouble so he'll want her in hospital. Angus is very anxious about it all and wondering if he should have allowed her to get pregnant. Marjorie thinks it happened on the night after they'd seen The Mikado. She's over the moon of course, hospital or no hospital.'

Not really wanting Pearl's version of how and when they might have got Marjorie pregnant, I grasped my opportunity in a different direction, 'Where does she live then, Pearl, what hospital will she go to?'

'Well, they live in Furlingdene – a beautiful old house, all covered with ivy and wisteria – so Wharton's her nearest hospital, unless she goes private and then I suppose she'll go to Birmingham.' Pearl's face could go from sheer delight to joy-crushing primness faster than ought to have been possible, and did so now, 'Angus will want to do what's best for her and the baby of course.'

I'd never heard of Furlingdene, but wasn't at all surprised to hear from Pearl that it was one of the best (and poshest, of course) villages around Wharton. I looked forward to a Saturday afternoon stroll with Pat in the not too distant future.

Meanwhile I was keen for the next phone call from Marjorie. She didn't disappoint and rang the very next day. I'd already asked Pearl if I was supposed to know the happy news and been reassured that although they weren't telling *anybody* just yet, it was fine that she, Pearl, had told me. We were special. After all, Pearl was going to be a Godmother. So after reassuring Marjorie as usual that Pearl seemed in the best of health and spirits, I offered my congratulations.

'Oh thank you Alice, we're *so* happy and excited! Of course it's very early days but I expect the time will fly by, and I'm *so* looking forward to holding my own baby, mine and Angus's.'

Without pausing to wonder how she'd respond, I rather cheekily said, 'You'll have to bring the baby in to show me when you're back on your feet.'

'Oh… yes… of course.' What else could she say? *'Not on your life – we don't really exist'?*

'Are you hoping for a boy or a girl? Or don't you really mind?' I was getting bolder.

Unsurprisingly she mouthed the usual rubbish about it not mattering in the slightest, 'as long as baby is healthy', and we ended the call. And once again, I didn't mention the call to Pearl, and hardly bothered to wonder why not.

That afternoon passed in a flurry of 'gone-again' gossip, knitting patterns for baby clothes ('we can't knit anything yet,' Pearl stated firmly, 'it's unlucky to get baby things before at least three or four months have passed') and the inevitable round sliced milk loaf from Wimbushes. Just another day at the office, really.

THIRTEEN

My weekend in Southsea arrived, so Marjorie and Angus (now abbreviated to 'Mangus' by Pat) completely disappeared from my consciousness. As planned, I took Friday as a day of annual leave and caught the first coach of the day from Birmingham going south. It took all day, including two changes with long waits in between, but I didn't really mind; I had my *Pilgrim Cottage Omnibus* to read but mostly I spent the journey alternating between making my plans for Saturday and working up enhancements of possibilities for The Game. I found a nice enough affordable B&B quickly through the conveniently located Chamber of Commerce right outside the bus station, although the landlady probed a bit too much for my comfort level on why I was here just for two nights and one day to go to the theatre, and on a Saturday afternoon at that.

'Surely you have theatres in the Midlands?'

'Well, yes, of course we do, but I'm a dedicated Gilbert and Sullivan fan, so I go all over the country to see them.' I tried to look as if this was the most natural thing in the world, but in reality I was rather embarrassed and certainly didn't want to say I was actually a fanatical follower of The New Savoyards, particularly Helen Easton and Matthew Dexter. Nor did I feel like offering any information about not being able to afford an evening performance as well as accommodation and travel, but she could probably guess that anyway. I don't think too many well-heeled tourists laid their heads on the rubber pillows at *Chez Belle Maison,* where the landlady apparently never took her curlers out.

She shook her head disapprovingly and the plastic rollers rattled, 'Well it's not for me to say, but a young girl like you... I should have thought you'd have better things to spend your money on.'

I smiled, enigmatically I hoped, and she sniffed. 'Well, I never did.'

Well, she didn't have to, and no, it was not for her to say. I was in Southsea on a mission, and I had Things to Do on

Saturday morning: I had to find No. 137 Ivyleaf Lane and No. 14 Braxton Court. But partly to appease her and partly because there wasn't anything else to do, I took an evening stroll along the beach finishing the sandwiches I'd brought from home to save money. Then I turned in for an early night. Tomorrow was going to be busy.

I decided not to ask the landlady where these streets were, but instead got directions from her for the library, where I hoped there would be useful street maps. If she thought it odd I was going to the library on a lovely sunny Saturday morning in a seaside town, she didn't say so, but in any case I was past caring. I think she'd already slotted me into the category of 'odd' – but then she probably saw so many strange people coming through her guesthouse that it would have to have been really outrageously weird behaviour to register more than momentarily. I wondered idly, as I strode up to the library, what she'd make of Pearl. Hmm, come to think of it, what would Pearl make of her? What kind of a life story would she spin around the unsuspecting woman permanently in curlers who opened her home to all and sundry? Pearl would probably 'fall in love' with her. She seemed to 'fall in love' with half the population of people she knew – or knew of. I wondered if that was also a result of her wonderfully romantic love affair with Cyril coming to naught?

The library came through for me and I was outside No. 137 by quarter past ten. On minimal evidence, I decided immediately that this was the right place, Helen Easton's parents' home, so I wouldn't need to walk miles to the other side of town to Braxton Court. That was quite a relief, as it was an unusually warm day.

It was an unremarkable house but looked, I was convinced, lived in by well-loved (posh, of course) and loving people. I admired its red brick courtyard as I walked slowly past, then turned at the end of the street to walk back the other way. I don't know what I thought I might see, or what I would do next – I could hardly keep walking by and I certainly couldn't just stand there looking at the house. But as I was approaching for my second pass, I was just in time to see a dark blue Jaguar slide out of the drive and disappear down the street in the other direction, towards the town and out of sight.

I tried to memorise the number plate: a seven, a nine, maybe a nought – or a letter O – and a six? Were there two people in it? I thought so: a man and a woman. I also thought there might have been a child in the back seat. Bridget? Must be. But where were they taking her? They weren't 'ordinary' people, so they wouldn't be doing the normal things people do on a Saturday morning – like going shopping. Or, in Southsea, going to the beach. No, they'd be on their way to the theatre for the afternoon performance and surely Bridget would stay at home with her grandmother? Or maybe not, maybe she was going to spend the afternoon at a friend's house elsewhere in Southsea. After all, that's where she lived. So Mummy and Daddy were doing the parental thing and taking her there, then her granny, Helen's mother, would collect her at teatime and put her to bed, as usual.

I walked back to the B&B, congratulating myself on my luck at being at the right place at the right time (rather than on the other side of town at the Braxton Court address), and greatly looking forward to my lunch of fish and chips on the sea front. By the time I arrived at the theatre for the 2pm matinee of HMS Pinafore I had a firm picture in my mind of what I had seen: Matthew and Helen, chatting contentedly and lovingly to each other, with Bridget in the back seat. I began working on their likely conversation until the performance started.

I more than happily gave myself over to the entertainment, cheering loudly for more and more encores of *Never mind the why and wherefore,* soaking up how lovingly Sir Joseph Porter KCB (Matthew) looked at Hebe (Helen), and inventing still more little stories for our future Game activities. I wondered if the tenor playing Ralph Rackstraw (Arthur Bosworth) might have a thing for the lead soprano, Jane Hartford. And what about the conductor? He might be married to the contralto and they both would be sort of surrogate parents for Helen and Matthew when they were on tour. Would Helen's actual parents resent that, or would they be grateful and actually have regular phone conversations with the older couple about their very sensitive daughter and her wonderfully loving husband? Lots and lots of rich and juicy scenarios to be worked up and played out. I hoped I wouldn't forget any, but didn't really think I would. I never had.

After the performance I hung around the stage door for a while, hoping I wasn't as pathetic-looking as the half a dozen or so other assorted and mostly scruffy souls waiting there. Eventually the doorkeeper stuck his head out and said, not unkindly, 'Nobody'll be coming out you know, they've got another performance to prepare for.' Disconsolately we melted away in our various directions, but my disappointment didn't last long; to my utter delight and cementing my conviction that I had indeed seen my heroes that morning, I walked past a dark blue Jaguar parked in a side street not far from the theatre. There were no sevens, nines or noughts on the number plate (though there was a six) but after all, I hadn't been able to see it too well that morning anyway. I almost danced my way back to the fish and chip van on the sea front, feeling so completely emotionally satisfied that for the first time in ages I wasn't accompanied by imaginary Bruce to bed in the hot and stuffy little room on the top floor of the B&B.

I didn't give Bruce a thought on the coach trip back to the Midlands either. Remembering our success in getting a nice letter and photograph from the conductor Paul Mullins, I decided that we, Pearl and I, might just as well write to Matthew and Helen and ask them for a photograph. Would it be too cheeky to ask for one of them together? I thought we might risk it, and spent the first leg of the journey crafting the letter in my head. (Pearl would want it to include Bridget, but I drew the line at asking for that!) I thought I'd write to Arthur and Jane, as well as the conductor and his contralto wife, and start a nice collection of Savoyard photographs. I'd invest in a handsome album to keep them in, and it would *not* have 'People I love' embossed on the front.

I also spun the story of my Southsea adventures, embellished the saga of my inquisitive landlady – who'd paid me practically no attention at breakfast, and was still in her curlers – and worked on my version of our Game. I looked forward to Monday morning and Pearl's ready ear for all I had to tell.

And when all that palled for a moment, I got stuck into the *Pilgrim Cottage Omnibus*. It was hard going though, and I skipped quite a bit; I was up to Chapter IV of the second book and it had really not grabbed me at all. I thought I might have to give up after all. Cecil Roberts, the author, was turning out to be a bit of a lifter of good phrases himself; his caricature (unintentional, I'm sure) of a world-famous pianist (whose hitherto unacknowledged illegitimate daughter by a world-famous opera singer is clearly going to be the sappy heroine of this volume) dies melodramatically at the end of Chapter III, and his final words are 'light – more light – more light'. I'm pretty sure I remember my father years ago struggling to mend a standard lamp using that exact phrase and telling me they were Goethe's final words. I'd have to ask him when I got home – except that I was not really speaking to him, or him to me. I'd ask my mother to ask him instead; I needed to know. Things like this were unsettling to me. Had I not been so obsessed in the moment with Helen and Matthew and The Game, I might have wondered what mad parallel universe I'd wandered into. In hindsight, I probably should have wondered.

On the last leg of my journey there was an unexpected bonus. We made an unscheduled stop for a greatly embarrassed but desperate lady to use the bathroom in a charming half-timbered pub where I spotted on the sign over the door that the proprietor was one Mark Ivan Edward Dexter. I immediately put the *Omnibus* away and set about making Mark Ivan Edward Dexter a brother to Matthew Dexter – probably one of three brothers, I thought, all four being named after the Gospels. The other two, younger (Matthew would be the oldest), would of course be Luke and John. They needed wives, perhaps children, jobs, personalities... This was almost my favourite part of playing The Game; something I could and did do by myself, although Pearl was certainly a willing participant when allowed to join in. From time to time I wondered if she'd had a similar kind of experience growing up as I had in this arena: I'd spent hours walking around the village, along the canal path and over the fields, creating whole families with back stories and fascinating conflicts and dilemmas. I was rarely me, Alice Chorley; I was somebody else, anybody in the created family, but always 'good', clever, pretty, well-loved and – most important of all – understood and reassured by perpetually understanding and reassuring people.

So Mark Ivan Edward Dexter, along with his newly invented brothers, was glorious fodder for The Game, and I made sure (as she would say) that Pearl would be a willing participant when I got back to the office.

FOURTEEN

How wrong I was! Pearl was not, apparently, particularly interested in anything I had to say on Monday morning. She was in a strange mood; droopy, monosyllabic, yet at the same time saying over and over how relieved she was to have me back safe and well, and acting as if she wanted to hug me. (She never had, but I was always aware that it was never very far away, so I never felt quite relaxed in her presence.) I couldn't work out what had happened or what might be wrong with her. She was 'fine', she said tightly, when I asked. Marjorie was 'as well as can be expected', and everything was all right at home with Mother. I asked how Friday had gone for her without me there, had anything happened? No. It was all 'fine'. Had she had to fetch the bread for the Stevens family? No, Edna Betty hadn't rung. How about 'gone-again'? No, he hadn't. My at first lively telling of my Southsea weekend quickly petered out when there was no interested response from Pearl, so I limped to a halt before I even got to the bit about Matthew's pub-owning brother.

I gave up, disappointed and angry. She'd *ruined* my happy weekend and over what? She obviously wasn't going to tell me, so I turned my attention to the stationery cupboard, giving it a much needed tidy-up and clear out. As I worked, noisily and somewhat unnecessarily dramatically, I planned what I might say to Marjorie if she were obliging enough to ring at lunchtime. 'No, your brave and noble lovely Pearl is *not* fine, and I have no idea what's wrong, but it's pretty grim in the office this morning, I can tell you.'

Marjorie didn't ring, but Pearl seemed to restore herself during her lunch, coming perilously close – again – to hugging me on her return, and apologising over and over again for 'dumping my sorrows on you, dearest Alice. You didn't deserve that.' I tried to be gracious, but my heart wasn't in it, so when Pearl asked enthusiastic questions about my weekend and all that had happened I wasn't very forthcoming. Her rapid change in behaviour felt like another game and one I absolutely did not want to play.

'So you're positive you saw Bridget in their car, Alice?'

I shrugged, 'Who knows, really. All I can be sure of was that I saw a car that could have been theirs and I think there was a child in the back seat.' I saw her flinch, but gamely she tried again.

'I'll bet they took her to the theatre with them. They'd want her to have a flavour of their life and being in Southsea, this was the perfect opportunity. They probably let her stay for the performance... Oh, I'll bet Helen's mother and father came for the performance and sat with Bridget too. Oh Alice, just think, you were in the theatre at the same time as not only Helen and Matthew, but also her parents and Bridget.' Pearl's eyes sparkled.

I shrugged again. 'We'll never know.' I was still angry and wanted to make her work for a share in my weekend pleasure. I still held back the bit about 'brother' Mark; she'd have to work a bit harder before I gave her that, nasty little thing that I was. Nor was I going to tell her about the letter I'd drafted for us to send to Helen and Matthew. At least not yet. Maybe I'd send it and *then* tell her, when or if I got a response. Maybe. And I'd certainly leave her name off it. I might even not tell her about the other letters I was planning to write and send. It was dawning on me that I could be a groupie on my own; I didn't need any collaboration or encouragement from Brenda Pearl Taylor. In fact, it might be better without her.

The afternoon wore on. Rather earlier than usual, Edna Betty rang for her sliced milk loaf which I duly fetched and, unusually for him, Officer Hampton – having seen my industrious attack on the stationery cupboard – asked if I would help him with some sorting out of things in his office, and I was glad to do it. The atmosphere in our office felt very uncomfortable, despite Pearl's apparent emotional recovery, which felt somehow quite false.

Officer Hampton turned out to be rather charming, a bit old-worldly and quite given to strange turns of phrase, but as we talked about this and that while we worked together, I saw another side of him and found that I actually really liked him. He was interested in my visit to Southsea, although not, he said, himself a Gilbert and Sullivan fan. He wanted to know if

I'd visited the castle: 'Built in 1544,' he said excitedly, 'as part of Henry VIII's fortification against the invasion of Britain, which I won't bore you with for the moment. But it's well worth a visit if you ever return there.' He revealed a dry sense of humour, a touching faith in 'the best in people', and a serious passion for choral music (though not Gilbert and Sullivan) and cricket. 'And I hope I never have to choose between them, for I wouldn't know how to make such a decision.' He looked quite stricken at the possibility and I searched my brain to think of a situation where he might be called upon to make such a choice. I felt unpleasant pangs of guilt for having laughed at his perpetual cheerfulness and vowed not to judge people so hastily ever again. Bless him, he even, somehow, managed to get me to say something like that before the afternoon with him was over. If he knew I was referring to him, albeit obliquely, he was kind enough not to let on. I suspect he'd been laughed at quite a bit in his life and I felt very uncomfortable and mean at my part in that. He was a small, rotund man and had doubtless been horribly teased and bullied as a child, but somehow he'd managed to maintain his optimistic view of the world. I felt a huge surge of warmth towards him, and not just because he'd rescued me from the oppressive atmosphere in our office. I hoped his wife really loved him and enjoyed choral music and cricket with him.

Going back downstairs I thought I might try to be a bit nicer to Pearl, too, but not before I had laid down my marker about now having great liking and respect for Officer Hampton. 'You know what? I really enjoyed that – he's quite sweet and was very easy to work with.'

She took it like a lamb, nodding quickly and dislodging one of her garishly floral earrings, but not really seeming not to notice before beginning yet another apology for her morning misery. 'I haven't wanted to tell you this Alice, I know you're going to be so upset, but I can't hide it from you any longer... You're very intuitive, you always *know* when something's wrong, no matter how well I hide it.'

Hide it? She couldn't have flagged up her distress more plainly if she'd carried a screaming placard. Irritated all over again I stared at her. '*What*? Tell me Pearl, what on earth's happened?'

She leaned dramatically over her typewriter and mumbled, 'Marjorie something-mutter-something, and I didn't want you to be upset. But I knew you would be, so I've tried so hard to hide it...' She drooped even further over her desk, losing her remaining earring in the process. It fell to the floor and I briefly considered picking it up for her before realising I'd feel better if I stayed on my side of the room.

'Marjorie *what*? Pearl, please sit up and tell me what on earth has happened.' I couldn't imagine what it might be and was struggling hard to keep up my new resolution of being more forbearing with people, especially when they were being as sickeningly melodramatic and incomprehensible as Pearl.

'Oh Alice... she's lost the baby!' She put her head down on the desk and sobbed. Loudly and, I suspected with considerable distaste, wetly. I fervently hoped for her sake that none of the officers chose that moment to appear in our office. I hoped it for my sake, too. If they came in I might have to actually go over to Pearl and make some attempt to comfort her for the sake of appearances.

But I was also stunned. 'Oh no! Oh Pearl, what happened?' It's interesting how the mind can operate on several tracks at once. Part of me was conscious of being absolutely repelled by Pearl's melodramatics, another part felt cheated, remembering her offhand response to my question about Marjorie that morning, but the greatest part of me was genuinely shocked at this news.

'It was on Friday. She started having pains on Thursday night so of course Angus rang the doctor. He came out straight away and did everything he could, but he couldn't save the baby. He only just managed to save Marjorie, she lost so much blood.' The sobbing had stopped and she actually spoke quite clearly.

'Oh God, I'm so sorry. That's awful, Pearl. I don't know what to say. Is she still in hospital?'

'No, she's at home, she was really too ill to be moved, and she's so weak and of course she's terribly, terribly sad. Angus says she just lies in bed with the curtains drawn listening to Wagner. He's beside himself with worry about her.'

'As well as his own disappointment, I suppose. Do they know why? Why she lost the baby?'

'The doctor has privately told Angus that Marjorie can't have children, she can't carry them to full term apparently, there's something wrong inside, but he hasn't told her that. They are both letting her believe there must have been something wrong with the baby so losing it was more of a blessing than anything else. He'll need to wait a while before he breaks that awful news to her. But I think he thinks she knows anyway.'

'Have you seen her?' I tried to stay in the present, but was already thinking of Angus lovingly and with tremendous understanding telling Marjorie they could never have their longed-for babies. What a great scene for The Game that was going to be! (Though perhaps played out without Pearl, under the circumstances.) And when she got over it a bit, they could adopt. Twins! Silent twins who'd been so traumatised in a place like the Swansea orphanage that it took all the McIntoshes' love and care and understanding reassurance to bring them out. And when they did speak, they'd call Angus 'darling', because that's the only thing they'd ever heard Marjorie call him. And they'd...

'Oh no, she's much too ill. She can't have visitors for a long time, but when she's up to it, Angus will come and fetch me so I can see her. Meanwhile of course I'm praying for her and yesterday I lit a candle in our church. Two actually, one for her and one for the baby's soul.'

'How about one for Angus? He's flipping heroic – again!'

She sniffed and looked offended at the implied criticism. 'Well of course it was for Marjorie *and* Angus. You know that, Alice.'

The day – the day that I had looked forward to so much and turned out to be so very different – came to an end and I went home. My mother was out, enjoying one of her fortnightly whist drives in the village hall, where she would probably win another box of slightly off chocolates or a hundred stale cigarettes for my father that he'd sneer at but smoke anyway, so I rang Pat to offload.

'Murderer!' She giggled.

'Who? What do you mean? *Me*? Why?'

'You killed that baby, Alice. The poor little sod was doomed the moment you got Marge to agree to bring it into the office.'

'Oh shit, I never thought of that.' My brain split again; this time half was still on the shock and horror of the loss of the baby and the other half busy recognising that Pat's conviction that there was no Marjorie – and therefore of course no baby – had just got another boost.

FIFTEEN

Pearl and I never spoke about the scenes, how they would play themselves out. We never seemed to plan them, either. They just evolved, unlike when I was younger and used to play 'grown-ups' with my then friend Maureen and her fabulous giant dressing-up box of her glamorous mother's cast-off clothes (the major reason for my friendship with her, actually). Unlike Pearl and me now, we'd spend quite a bit of the playtime on preliminaries and plans, setting up the scenario to make sure we were both satisfied.

''Tend we're two working girls sharing a flat in London and you come home late from work and find me unconscious on the sofa with an empty pill bottle, cos I thought they were sweets and ate them all.'

'Yes, then 'tend I dial 999...'

'... and a handsome doctor comes and saves my life and then he falls in love with me.'

'No, he falls in love with *me*, loving me for rescuing you and calling 999 – *you're* a mess, you've been sick, he wouldn't fall in love with *you.'* (Ah Maureen, you don't know the Cyril Brownes and Angus McIntoshes of this world.)

One exception to this no-planning unspoken rule was Helen and Matthew's 'wedding night'. The next time Pearl's mother went to Wales by herself we decided to treat ourselves to a Saturday overnight stay in Malvern, coming back on Sunday. We both knew this was a good opportunity for a serious scene, so while neither of us actually said ''tend it's their honeymoon', I did venture a broader-than-usual hint: 'could be the first night of the honeymoon...' and Pearl nodded enthusiastically. 'Oh yes!' before whipping out the bus timetables for Westfield to Malvern, via Birmingham.

'I've been longing to show you my lovely Malvern.' Pearl usually claimed ownership of places she'd especially liked – actually just about anywhere she'd been – and this was turning out to be another of her idiosyncrasies that irritated me and left me feeling dissatisfied with the person I seemed to be becoming. For all her apparently unconditional adoration of me, being around her really didn't make me like myself very much. Pat, on the other hand, with her occasional barbs and criticisms, oddly did more for my self-esteem than Pearl's steady diet of undying and totally unremitting love. I did occasionally wonder why that was; perhaps it had something to do with the fact that as stupid/difficult/childish as Pat sometimes said I was, she still wanted to be my friend; that had to count for something. Or perhaps with Pearl and me it was the Groucho Marx thing – he was reputed to have said he wouldn't want to belong to any club that would have him as a member. Nobody had found me particularly wonderful before, so there must be something wrong with Pearl to think so highly of me.

I didn't count Jack; he'd been on the rebound from Wendy Freeman and had *needed* me to salve his wounded ego. He was doubtless as relieved – in the end – as I was that we were no longer seeing each other. I managed to maintain this view despite my mother telling me she'd seen him walking through the village on the Sunday afternoon I was coming back from Southsea, wearing the rather naff green sleeveless pullover I'd so lovingly knitted for him. There had to be a message in that as he'd been considerably less than enthusiastic when I'd given it to him and had only worn it once, very briefly, in my presence. I hadn't been surprised; it was far from perfectly constructed, though I definitely didn't appreciate the information he'd later passed on from his mother that I'd done the increase of stitches all wrong. 'She says you're supposed to add stitches more gradually, Spud, not all at once at the waistline.' My shame was made worse by knowing she was right, but of course I couldn't let Jack see that. How dare she, ignorant woman that she was, know more about the finer points of knitting than I did?

We set off for Malvern on a dull Saturday afternoon, after we'd both been on duty at the office until 1pm. There had been no work at all to do, so we'd spent the morning drinking coffee, eating buns Pearl had brought in from home, and talking about how lovely the Malvern Hills would be at this time of year. It took the better part of the afternoon to get there and when we did, rather than go exploring or walking in the lovely hills, Pearl said we had to find a B&B. She took charge;

she and her mother did this kind of thing regularly, she said, but – and I suppose for obvious reasons – she didn't want to use their usual B&B.

The first one we tried was a no-go; the landlady flatly refused to show us any of her rooms, saying rather harshly, 'we're full!' as she ripped the 'Vacancies' sign off the door.

Pearl was very upset: 'Upset for *you,* dear Alice,' she kept saying. I didn't really know why, but then I didn't really know why the landlady had thought there was anything wrong with a middle-aged woman and a late-teens girl having a weekend away together, so I was inclined to believe that she was indeed full.

The next one was fine, although I was a bit put out when the landlady asked us if we wanted one or two beds and I said, mindful of The Game we were planning, 'Oh one, that way we'll be warmer', and Pearl glared at me, mouthing '*shush*!' Didn't she *want* us to share a bed? I was hurt and had half a mind to sulk when I saw we had two single beds, but decided not to; there was nothing to be gained in this instance. My sulks needed quite a bit more than half a day to get resolved, so there wasn't really time for one now.

We deposited our bits of luggage and set off for what turned out to be a rather damp and chilly walk in what I thought were distinctly *un*lovely Malvern Hills. Pearl said it was too soon to go back to the B&B so we sat a bit miserably in a dreary teashop for a couple of hours over a single cup of horribly stewed tea each, and then moved on to get some fish and chips, which we ate standing up in a bus shelter, watching the rain run down its grubby windows.

At eight fifteen Pearl said we could begin to make our way slowly back to the B&B. Good! I was beginning to think this whole adventure had been a complete waste of time and energy.

We'd played The Game spasmodically on the bus, on the walk, and eating our fish and chips. Naturally they hadn't been fish and chips in our Game; Grilled Dover sole and Lyonnaise potatoes are what the newly married Helen and Matthew ate, sitting in a very posh restaurant of course, and drinking champagne. It may well have been raining, but they wouldn't have cared, and they wouldn't have been looking out of dirty windows, either.

Back at the B&B, which was now a five star hotel in the Algarve, I used the communal toilet on the landing first, with its ineffectual hanging bunch of lavender, and then slid quickly into my utilitarian pyjamas and into bed whilst Pearl was out of the room. I never liked using a toilet after her; she frequently left an unpleasant smell and often traces of her activity in there. (No wonder Mother didn't like her using their bathroom.) Upon her return she made a big performance of washing at the sink in our room, her mannish striped pyjama jacket unbuttoned to the waist and revealing very unpleasant-looking flattened and flapping breasts that she clearly wanted me to see and comment on. I didn't; I pretended, even to myself I realised later, not to notice, turned onto my side and wondered how The Game was going to progress from here.

Pearl, as Matthew, lay beside me on my narrow bed and said all the right things. My lovely frisson returned to make it a pleasure for me but I was more than a bit startled when she suddenly threw herself on top of me making grunting noises and simulating humping me, but it didn't last long. She then moved back to her bed, still firmly in role, and continuing to say all the right things for Matthew to have said to Helen after their first married coupling. I said nothing – as either Helen or me, Alice; I was shocked into a paralysing numbness.

Somehow this was all a step too far for me. Frissons or not, I couldn't dislodge the thought that we must be really weird to be doing this. I had no idea if Pearl had the same kind of frisson as I did; we never discussed that either, so I don't know what, if anything, she got out of it. She must have got something; playing The Game was as much at her instigation as mine. But maybe she wanted something else, something more. I certainly didn't. I wasn't even sure if I wanted this any more. We seemed to have crossed at least two lines with this episode: we'd never before really planned a scene, and we'd never before had any actual physical contact in The Game. The former probably wasn't important, but finding Pearl as repulsive as I did, I definitely didn't want the latter. In those moments she had ceased to be Matthew to me and had very definitely been Pearl. And I didn't like it at all. My father's comment impugning Pearl's sexual orientation – albeit passed on by my mother, so quite possibly not completely accurate – came back to me. I hadn't paid a lot of attention at the time because I knew my father was given to making disparaging remarks about anybody and everybody. But if he'd been right, and Pearl was lesbian or had lesbian tendencies, how had she managed to fall in love with Cyril? Was it possible to fancy both men and women? It was all too much for my nineteen-year-old brain so, exhausted and confused, I drifted off to a very restless sleep as the relentless rain battered against the window.

SIXTEEN

Out of nowhere, I suddenly remembered in the first volume of the *Pilgrim Cottage Omnibus,* the sappy romantic couple eating crumpets by the fire. Even that early on I was already skipping huge chunks of the book, so I hadn't paid it a great deal of attention. Now, however, I had a strong urge to find that part and read it properly.

Cursing my previous impatience, I searched each page, looking for the scene. And there, at the bottom of page 145, it was:

'Darling, your fingers are greasy!' protested Ann.

'Sorry – so's your mouth, little Miss Muffet!'

I felt sick. *Could* it have been just a coincidence? It was hard to see how; Miss Muffet was famous for eating her curds and whey, not crumpets, and crumpets were what both couples (Philip and Ann, Matthew and Helen) had been eating. Clearly Pearl had modelled her stories of Helen and Matthew (and Angus and Marjorie?) on the couples in Pilgrim Cottage, but why on earth had she urged me to read it? Did she think I wouldn't recognise the words she had given to Helen and Matthew? Or had she somehow stored the scene (as well as the poignant Russian farewell) in her brain and then forgotten where she'd got it? Perhaps she was going dotty faster than I realised. And if I continued reading, would I come across a longed-for pregnancy followed by a life-threatening miscarriage? And worse: was I in danger of becoming like Pearl and forgetting what was real and what was fantasy?

I also felt sick with the knowledge that I wasn't going to confront her about it, either. I briefly imagined doing that, but knew I wouldn't be able to tolerate watching her squirm as she somehow managed to lie her way out of it whilst making me, somehow, the villain for asking and doubting. She might even say that as Marjorie had also read the *Pilgrim Cottage* books, *she* had been the one to steal the incident and pass it on to Pearl. I knew I couldn't face that, so instead I rang Pat to set up our expedition to Furlingdene for the coming Saturday.

I was in two minds about whether or not to tell Pat about this latest discovery. By itself it was nothing but good evidence for Pat's conviction that Pearl was a complete fantasist – a conclusion I was having an increasingly hard time ignoring – but I could see how it could easily lead to questions from Pat about how the conversation had arisen in the first place. I couldn't let Pat know about The Game, nor how complicit I had been with Pearl's fantasy activities. That would have been entirely too shaming. But, and this was a big but, I was beginning to doubt my own sanity where Pearl was concerned, so a bit of Pat's down to earth common sense could be a useful dose of normality. I could probably tell her the tale of the greasy crumpets if I were careful, I decided, without revealing anything about The Game and my part in it.

It was my Saturday in the office, but not Pearl's, so I didn't have to hide what I was doing and where I was going after work. Pearl probably wouldn't have asked anyway, she would have assumed I was going home as usual, but I feared my guilt might show and I wouldn't be able to deal with it. I met Pat at the bus stop, where we caught the one fifteen to Wharton. Pat only 'sort of knew' where Furlingdene was, so I was quite relieved to see a sign on the only bus standing in the bus station in Wharton saying 'Fillshall via Furlingdene'. And evidently neither place was particularly popular, as we were the only people on the bus apart from the heavily Brylcreemed conductor.

'Where to, ladies?' He snapped his ticket holder and smiled at us. Well, he smiled at Pat, anyway.

'Two day returns to Furlingdene, please,' Pat was obviously in charge.

'Day returns? When you ladies coming back then? You won't get a bus back to Wharton now till Monday.'

Pat didn't miss a beat. 'OK, two singles to Furlingdene then, please. And will you tell us when we get there?' She gave him the money; he smiled beatifically at her and gave her the two tickets. I might as well not have even been there for all the notice he took of me. Which was not an unusual occurrence when I was out with Pat. She was more than simply attractive; she had *presence*. And she knew how to use it.

'How will we get back?' I was irritated now. Was I the only one in touch with any kind of reality? I certainly hadn't fancied the bus conductor, but it would have been nice at least to have been acknowledged.

'We'll use their phone to ring Alan. What's the point of having a boyfriend if he won't come and fetch us on a Saturday afternoon?'

Slightly reassured, I gave myself over to our detecting adventure. We got off the bus at the village green that could have come straight off a calendar of *Beautiful Villages of Britain* with its pond, complete with quacking ducks, and a floral display to rival the Chelsea Flower Show.

'Told you it was posh.' Pat looked round approvingly. 'Oh look! It won Best-Kept Village in 1956; wonder what's happened since then. The competition must be really tough. Right, I suggest we pop in the pub and ask strategic questions. We haven't got all day.'

Fortunately for Pat's plans the pub was open, though of course not serving alcohol until six o'clock. We each had a glass of lemonade and a packet of crisps and set about quizzing the owner on what sort of people lived in Furlingdene.

'Retired folk, mostly. Retired professionals, with money.'

'And professional people still working – perhaps in Wharton?' Pat fluttered her heavily mascara-laden lashes at him.

'Might be. Don't know of any though.' He turned back to washing up the lunchtime glasses, apparently immune to Pat and her dark lashes.

Pat evidently decided not to be coy any longer. Actually, I'd noticed that about her before – she knew when not to bother, and would probably say later that the landlord was 'queer'. It would never occur to her that somebody simply might not fancy her. I envied that. 'Do you know the McIntoshes? Angus and Margaret, I think it is, though it might be Andrew and Marjorie, or even Angus and Marjorie. I'm not quite sure.' She winked at me, mouthing 'pansy'.

He shook his head. 'Newcomers? Or maybe non-drinkers, in which case I probably wouldn't know them. Though we get a fair few of them nowadays. Why don't you have a look at the Parish Register? If they live in Furlingdene they'll be listed there. Friends of yours, are they?'

Ignoring his curiosity – surely we'd know their names if they were our friends – we asked for directions to the church which, just like the village green, looked as if it belonged on a chocolate box or in a picture book of *Glorious England.*

'They're a lot more trusting in Furlingdene than they are in Westfield', Pat observed as we went through the wide-open huge wooden door. There was no one around to grant or deny permission to look at the Parish Register, which sat conveniently on a table just inside the vestibule, so we helped ourselves. Of course there was no listing for any McIntosh, Angus and Marjorie, or Andrew and Margaret, or indeed any McIntosh of any description on the Parish Roll for Furlingdene. The closest it came was a Miss Geraldine MacDonald, and no other 'Mc's' of any kind.

'Shit!' Pat slammed the massive book shut, 'I should have rung Alan from the pub. Well let's start walking back towards Wharton and when we find a phone box I'll ring him from there. And that's that.' She took a deep breath. 'Convinced now?' She seemed half triumphant and half irritated so, hoping to appease her, I decided to tell her about little Miss Muffet. She didn't ask any awkward questions, just pursed her lips and shook her head. 'You've got to get out of there, Alice. Working with a nut case like Pearl isn't good for your mental health. You're going to end up like her if you're not careful. You need a boyfriend anyway, not an old maid to play with.'

'I'm sure you're right, but chance would be a fine thing though.' I didn't really want to look for another job, though I certainly wanted to *be* in another and thereby away from Pearl. As for finding a boyfriend: not too likely in my current situation. Men like Angus (or Matthew… and Bruce) were a bit thin on the ground everywhere, but especially in Westfield Council environs.

We found a phone box eventually and boyfriend Alan was duly pressed into service to drive to Furlingdene to collect us. He, understandably, wasn't terribly happy about this, and unlike me – I would have worked my hardest to mollify him – Pat took this as an unforgiveable insult and sulked for the entire drive back to Westfield where they dropped me at the bus station. I had to wait almost an hour for a bus home and felt, when I finally got there, aggrieved with Pat, aggrieved with Alan, aggrieved with Pearl and, most of all, aggrieved with Marjorie and Angus who probably didn't even exist.

SEVENTEEN

In the same way that The Game had evolved into being, so it now evolved out of being: without a word from either Pearl or me. After our weekend in Malvern I promised myself – and rehearsed my 'speeches' endlessly – that I would tell Pearl I wasn't going to do it any more. But as usual, I bottled it, said nothing, and scolded myself on a daily basis for my weakness. I told myself I was waiting for Pearl to start a scene and I'd say something then. 'I don't want to do this any more,' was the phrase I'd planned, stated as firmly as I could manage and, taking advice from a magazine article I'd read recently on how to be assertive, repeating just that phrase until Pearl understood I really was no longer going to play. But Pearl never began another scene. Perhaps she sensed my distaste, or perhaps she'd got what she'd wanted in Malvern and no longer needed to play. Or maybe she'd been disappointed in my response (or lack thereof) and had given up on me as a player. I didn't know, and I didn't really care; I was just relieved we weren't playing and that I didn't actually have to say anything.

We didn't talk about The New Savoyards any more, and nor did Angus and Marjorie get much air time, but Pearl the Romantic was still going strong. There wasn't anything left to tell me about Cyril, but she suddenly introduced a 'dear friend of Cyril' into the equation and naturally he wanted to marry Pearl although of course he hadn't actually said so yet. In an eerie re-run of the Henry business, she told me, almost word for word the same, how she 'just *knew*' he was planning to ask her, but her heart was true to Cyril so she couldn't even contemplate it. 'But I can't bear to hurt him...' she sighed. 'He's such a good person and he loved Cyril so much. Cyril really loved him, too; they were like brothers. I love him too, as a dear, dear friend of Cyril's, but that's all. Somehow it would be fitting for us to marry, but it just isn't *right* and I can't do it.'

It's a good thing we weren't talking about Helen and Matthew because this new arrival on the adoration-of-Pearl scene was also called Matthew and it might have been quite confusing. For a person with such an active imagination, I'd have thought she could have come up with a different name... but, then again, maybe he was real; sometimes real people do have the same name, especially a fairly common name like Matthew. I really didn't know; my sense of reality seemed to have taken a rather large thumping lately.

I did urge Pearl to think hard before refusing him, though. I mean, how many more chances was she going to get? (Oh arrogant youth! And who was I to talk anyway? I didn't even have *one* man itching to marry me.) Her response was always that she couldn't countenance being unfaithful to Cyril's memory. I tried for compassion and patience. 'I don't know much about these things, Pearl, but it seems to me after more than five years you might at least think about starting to give yourself permission to come back to life a bit.'

It would have been perfectly understandable if she'd been annoyed at my crassness and told me to shut up, but no, she bowed her head meekly and said 'You're probably right dear Alice. So for you – and with your help – I'll try. I really will. And you must help me.'

That actually made it worse for me. I didn't want to be responsible for her resurrection, and I definitely didn't want to help her achieve it, even if I knew how. But I smiled gamely and said, 'Well, give him a chance and see where it goes.'

'I will, I will. I promise.' She looked as if she'd burst into tears at any moment, so I changed the subject. Which wasn't easy; so many things felt off-limits or dangerous territory these days and I realised how little we actually had to talk about that wasn't Game-related. How on earth had I thought that we had a lot of interests in common? For example, Malvern was currently in the news on a daily basis as they were hosting an Edward Elgar Festival and Officer Hampton and his wife were going. I was afraid this might prompt Pearl to want to talk about our weekend there, but all she ever said about Malvern, and that only once, was 'What a shame the weather was so rotten for us, dear Alice. You didn't see my lovely Malvern at its best.' She was undoubtedly right; it had rained solidly the entire time we were there, and we'd wasted no time getting the bus back home on Sunday morning. Rain is fine when you have a cosy home to hunker down in, but unbearable if you're lodging in a B&B with a person you really don't enjoy being with.

Sometimes I felt my sanity lay in playing the detective, trying to get a firm hold on what was really going on with Pearl and what was just fantasy. How, for example, was Matthew in touch with her and she with him? She'd said many times she couldn't have post at home because her mother was so nosy, and if Mother didn't know about Cyril it was a fair bet she didn't know about Matthew. Yet the only personal post that ever came to the office for Pearl was letters from her many friends, all of which she read openly in front of me, quoting lavishly from each one to demonstrate how much they loved her and how much they cared and worried about her. So where was she getting her recent information about his feelings to her? In a surge of more than usual irritation with her, I asked her.

'Oh I see him at the Brownes,' was her answer to my carefully phrased but oh-so-casual question. That just raised more questions for me: when did she go to the Brownes if she couldn't go anywhere without Mother? And why hadn't she said anything about him to me before? As with Henry, I discovered they'd never been out on a date together, but had they actually spent any time alone? Getting answers from her felt like trying to nail custard to the wall; if she was brilliant at fantasy, she was even more brilliant at obfuscating.

All week she hinted broadly that on Friday she might be seeing Matthew and that if she did, that would be The Night when he declared his undying love for her. 'What are you doing with Mother?' I said, doing my best to hide my smirk.

'Oh, she always goes round to Aunty Gert's on a Friday, so she won't know I've been out. I always make sure to be back before her. See! I used "made sure" correctly!'

I'd never heard of Aunty Gert before either, so I ignored her triumph at 'getting it right' – which she actually hadn't; she'd said 'make sure', not 'made sure' – and carried on my detective work. 'I thought she never went anywhere without you, Pearl.'

'Oh Alice, don't be so literal. Of course she does. She went to Wales, remember? And to Leeds. She's been to Wales several times on her own, as a matter of fact. In any case, it's not that she won't go anywhere without me – it's that *I* can't go anywhere without *her*. As I've told you, Alice. It's fine for *her* to have a life of her own, but I can't. As I've told you.' Her head went up and down vigorously and both earrings looked horribly threatened.

I gave up. But when she was at lunch I looked in her office diary to see if she'd written anything about Friday evening and saw she'd pencilled in very faintly 'Matthew – (Brownes). More interestingly, for Monday she'd written, also in faint pencil, 'tell Alice about M'. Why on earth would she need a reminder if Friday was going to be so momentous? I felt in need of a hefty dose of Pat's common sense, so rang her to invite her to come to lunch as soon as possible.

After lunch Pearl sat drooping at her desk. I was familiar enough with this to know Something Big was coming and I could either delay it by asking what was wrong, so she could say unhappily 'nothing...', or I could carry on with my own pursuits and wait for her to tell me. I decided on the latter course, and sure enough it wasn't long before she said, 'I've brought something to show you, dearest Alice.'

I didn't have to feign interest; I had no idea what it might be, but I was keen to see it, whatever it was. Hopefully it would be an illuminating piece in this increasingly confusing jigsaw puzzle.

She sniffed a couple of times, and put on her 'brave' face. 'Cyril's dear lovely mother wrote to me a few weeks after he died and of course I've saved the letter. I want you to see it.'

I tried not to show my surprise as I took the creased and crinkled piece of paper from Pearl's trembling hand. It certainly *looked* old; the green ink was quite faded and there were dried splotches all over it that I assumed would be Mrs B's tears as she wrote it – or Pearl's as she read it. Or both.

'May I read it?'

'Of course you can, darling Alice. I want you to. That's why I've brought it.' She resumed her droop and, doing my best not to notice that, I took the letter to my desk, where I placed it tenderly on the wooden desktop and tried to smooth it out, the better to read it.

My dearest Pearl,

Oh my dear, what can I say? My heart is so heavy with my own pain, but that can never blind me to the Awful Grief that you are struggling with so bravely. It's so very, very hard for a mother to lose her only son – and such a treasured boy, too – but I ca'nt imagine how dreadful it must be for you to lose not only the person you love, but to lose your future too. Bernard and I were so happy when you and Cyril found each other, and we were so looking forward to having you as our daughter and then, eventually, your (and Cyril's) children as our first grandchildren. They would have been such special little ones with his and your genes!

You have been so very brave, Pearl dear. God has been very good to us, giving us such lovely children and then bringing you into our lives. I know He will not desert you in your lonely hours. Keep your heart open to Him, dearest Pearl, and you will heal.

In deepest sympathy and with love for always, Vera Browne.

There was no date and no return address. And why had she capitalised awful grief? (My mother wouldn't like that!) So Cyril's Dad was Bernard – had the Brownes in the phone book been listed as Browne, B? I couldn't remember. I'd have to look it up later. I half-focused on these details and half on wondering what on earth I was now going to say to Pearl. But I couldn't help noticing that the handwriting was *very* like Pearl's, and my eye kept returning to the centre of the first paragraph where 'can't' was written 'ca'nt'.

EIGHTEEN

'Perhaps it's a Westfield thing,' I suggested to Pat next day when she came round at my urging to have lunch at the office, bringing the inevitable though of course always welcome hot dogs. 'Perhaps they put the apostrophe in the wrong place as an affectation – or like they all pronounce tour as two-uh.'

'Don't be daft. I'm Westfield born and raised and I've *never* seen or heard such an ignorant thing. No, you pathetic donkey, face it: *Pearl* wrote the letter. What more proof do you want? Probably no more than a couple of weeks ago and I'll bet she's left it in the sun to fade the ink. Green ink fades very quickly anyway. Shame you couldn't run it through the copier, though. I'd love to have seen it.'

'Maybe Pearl saw how Cyril's mother spells it and has adopted it for herself – it's the sort of sicky thing she'd do you know.' Why was I so reluctant to see what was obvious? I was irritating myself, never mind Pat.

'Yeah, maybe. You believe what you want to believe,' Pat's scorn hurt. I wanted to say – but didn't, of course, 'it hurts me *here*'.

'Honestly, Alice, I think you're in real danger of becoming as warped as Pearl. Please, please, *please!* Start looking for another job. In fact, no, *find* another job. Prompto, as the not-very-lovely Miss Taylor would say. And meanwhile, let's have a look at her diary. There might be all sorts of clues in there; the Brownes' phone number for instance. Oh yes! Let's ring them and, oh I don't know, ask how Cyril is?'

'We don't need Pearl's diary for their phone number, they're in the book – if they're the Brownes with an e that live on Garden Road. I think they are, they're listed with the initial B – for Bernard I assume.' (I'd looked it up the minute Pearl had left the office to take dictation from Officer Stevens.) Somehow I didn't like the way this was going, but I did nothing to stop Pat pulling the diary out of Pearl's desk drawer.

'Well maybe the devious Pearl has also looked in the phone book, and when she saw the B knew she had to give him a name beginning with that.' She opened the diary. 'Hmm... West End Surgery number... Royal Theatre box office... Palace Theatre box office... Revd. Bliss – what a smashing name for a vicar – and... oh... tons of names that don't mean a thing to me. You?' Pat passed me the diary.

'No. But Pat! Look, she's rubbed out "Matthew" on Friday. But not "tell Alice about M" on Monday. What do you suppose that means?'

'How the hell should I know? My brain doesn't work like hers. Thankfully.' She riffled through the largely empty pages. 'Borr-ring. Just like Pearl and her life, really.'

With considerable relief on my part we put the diary back in the drawer and returned to the kitchen to clear up after our hot dog lunch. Pat left, urging me to get the evening paper on my way home to look for another job, and I promised I would.

Pearl didn't mention Matthew again until we were about to leave on Friday. 'Oh Alice,' she grabbed my arm, 'Alice, Alice, I'm in such a turmoil about seeing Matthew this evening.'

My heart sank. She obviously wanted reassurance or comfort or *something* from me, but selfishly, I was mostly anxious not to miss my bus, and didn't know what to say anyway. 'You'll be fine Pearl, just speak from your heart and it will be all right.' All these romantic novels with their 'meaningful' dialogue and advice were not entirely wasted on me. I thought about saying 'God will guide you', but couldn't quite get it out.

'Oh darling Alice, you are such a tower of strength for me to lean on. Thank you *so* much for your support. You're right of course, I'll be fine. I'll think of you and I'll be fine. See you on Monday dear Alice, and have a lovely weekend.'

So I did. I hardly gave Pearl a thought, except to think how lovely it was going to be when I could tell her I was leaving. It had occurred to me that the shock might bring on her asthma again, but I pushed the thought aside, telling myself I'd deal with that if and when it happened. And in any case, I would no longer be here to need to deal with it very much. I'd be very happy to send her daily get-well cards, from a distance. Of course, I didn't actually *have* another job yet, but after taking Pat's advice and buying the evening paper on Wednesday, I saw that there were plenty of possibilities now that I had some experience and office training.

But I was nowhere near cured of my groupie/stalker behaviour yet, and spent most of Sunday crafting what I felt were stunning letters to several other members of The New Savoyards as well as to three of my favourites at the Birmingham Rep. I also went to church, renewing my acquaintance with God and urging Him to demonstrate His pleasure in having me back by sending me a plum job. Preferably not in Westfield, and definitely in a situation with a healthy supply of eligible men, please.

Pearl's potential showdown – if that's what it was – with Matthew didn't come back to me until I was almost at work on Monday morning. Unusually for her, Pearl was late, but Officer Park was there, along with two large policemen, filling our office with their combined bulk. 'He's gone again' had indeed gone again, and this time the police were involved. Why they were at our premises I wasn't sure, but gallantly offered to make them all tea or coffee and managed to manoeuvre them into the conference room and out of our space. They stayed for most of the morning, which meant that when Pearl did arrive, more explanations were necessary and it didn't seem possible to ask her about Matthew. At least, that's what I told myself.

Just before lunch she was called up to Officer Stevens' office and when she came down she told me that Park's ghastly runaway son, Brian, had stolen the Wilsons' ancient car. 'Officer Park will be taking a short leave of absence to get this all sorted,' she said, both of us trying hard not to smile. 'Officer Stevens is not happy with the amount of time he's spent involving us in his personal life and that has to stop, he said.' She'd also learned that Gone-Again had managed to crash the thing into a row of parked cars and was now languishing in custody at the local police station. Which is why, of course, the police were at our office, creating their own little drama and forestalling Pearl's.

But alas, not for long. Right after lunch – during which I looked in her diary to find she had now rubbed out 'tell Alice about M' – Pearl assumed her customary dramatic droop position over her long-suffering typewriter and sighed. I affected not to notice, so she did it again. 'Oh Alice...'

'Didn't go well, then?' There was no way out of it, so I thought I might as well get it over.

'No. Poor darling Matthew, he cried when he asked me. He was so sweet, he said it would be a fitting memorial to Cyril for us to be together and that he'd promised Cyril he'd take care of me and now I wouldn't let him and that was breaking his heart. He even said we could have a celibate relationship, if that's what was concerning me; he just wants to take care of me. But that wouldn't be right, Alice, people who marry should have a healthy sexual relationship in God's eyes. Oh, I felt so terrible, Alice. Do you think I should have said "yes", even though it would feel so wrong to me? I keep wondering what Cyril would want me to do, but I think I know. He'd want me to follow my heart, don't you think?'

I could hardly believe that she, in her late thirties, was looking to me, not yet twenty, to give her absolution for her decision, but I assumed my best pep-talk stance, despite knowing she'd tell her friends, 'Alice *told* me I was doing the right thing'.

So, 'No, Pearl, you have to do what feels right to you. You can't go around saving the world – or marrying blokes you don't love because you feel sorry for them. In the end you aren't doing them any favours anyway; you'd only have made him unhappy because he wasn't making you happy.' It was a good speech, but I felt sick making it because it all felt like such a farce. Somehow I was still playing a game, another unacknowledged game, and I felt stupid – and used. 'I know you don't believe it, but he'll get over it, Pearl – and what's more important, you'll get over it.' I didn't believe *that* either.

NINETEEN

Pat saw all this as vastly entertaining. I tried to, and certainly did my best to pretend to her that I was just as amused as she was, but in reality it distressed me horribly. I'd had difficulty with people not being entirely truthful for as long as I could remember, but this sort of challenge to my reality – gaslighting, as I saw it: a syndrome I'd recently learned about from the 1940s film *Gaslight* – was something else. It made me think of an incident in my childhood: I was, I think, less than five years old and, going upstairs for some now unremembered reason, had seen my mother stick her bare bottom out of their bedroom door as I turned from the top stair and onto the landing. I was enchanted and probably had made some sound to indicate my joy. At any rate, she saw me there, retreated quickly and closed the bedroom door firmly.

I hugged that delight to myself all day. My mum was not a particularly playful woman, so this was very important. It was a rare and special moment just between us, something to treasure. But alas, being only four or five I couldn't hold it, so at teatime over the fish-paste sandwiches, rock cakes and weak milky tea, I informed my astonished brother that I'd seen Mum's bare bum that morning when she'd poked it out of her bedroom door. I smiled happily at her, inviting her to acknowledge the magic of the moment we'd shared that morning.

It's a bit of a cliché to say she was apoplectic, but she was. 'I most certainly did *not!*' she said firmly, going very red in the face. 'You are making that up, Alice, and you are *not* to say such things. That's a very wicked lie and I'm ashamed of you.'

I was stunned on several levels. I knew what I had seen and, for a very brief moment, I knew she was lying but such is the power of grownups and their ability to distort their children's reality that I very quickly succumbed to her assertion that I was lying, that I had imagined the whole thing. This was an easy out for her, as I was well known for not being particularly truthful. Perhaps few children that age have a good grasp on what is truth and what is not, but I had seemed to be making a career for myself as Alice-the-Liar and thereby painfully increasing my mother's on-going disappointment in her daughter.

Either shortly before or not long after the bare bottom incident, I had provided further justification for this label by telling a visiting lady friend of my mother's that the sheepskin rug in the hall was from a sheep my father had purchased so that I might have a lamb to play with.

'And when it didn't have any lambs, my father killed it,' I had confided to Mrs Judas – who naturally couldn't wait to pass this on to my mother. *Nobody* saw this as wishful thinking; nobody recognised the yearning of a lonely little four-or-five-year-old to have a lamb to love, cuddle and play with, and a father who would go to extraordinary lengths (even killing a non-lamb-producing sheep) for his little girl. I got a royal telling off and was sent in shame to Sunday School in the hope that I would somehow, magically, and with God's help, become 'a good girl'.

It didn't happen: rather, I apparently got God on my side and, when I was accused of lying about a local farmer's sheep dog, saying I'd seen a wolf, I was reputed to have said – in response to the parental order to ask God's forgiveness for lying – 'God said, "oh that's all right, Alice; I've often made the same mistake myself".' Doubtless the story was apocryphal, or at least exaggerated, but my father's repeated telling of it did nothing for my reputation, firmly establishing me as an untruthful child.

Thus my story of my mother's lapse in taste and decency was easily dismissed as one of Alice's fantasies. You don't have to be Sigmund Freud to see why Pearl's altered view of reality hit such a nerve with me and was actually anything but funny. Years later I wondered if perhaps my mother had thought it was my father coming upstairs, although I'm not at all sure he wasn't away on Army business at the time. That she might have thought it was my brother, only two years older than me... well, piss off Freud, we're not going there.

Some things changed in the office. While Pearl continued her unremitting adoration of me and almost everything I did, she and I never played The Game again. We didn't talk about

Helen and Matthew and we hardly ever talked about Angus and Marjorie. I was not invited to stay at Pearl's house again; nor did she ever pay a repeat visit to mine. When her mother made one of her irregular visits to Wales we – Pearl and I – went to the theatre or a concert, half-heartedly discussing letters we might (but never did) send to one or more of the artists. And yet a variant of The Game did continue, a different version, but one we'd played before: some hapless couple at the next table or in the next row in the audience would be singled out by Pearl and away she'd go, creating their life story. And because I knew we had practically nothing else to talk about, I would join in. It was always the same life story: ultra-loving couple; sexually shy wife with ever-understanding husband; possibly – if we had enough time – interfering in-laws on one side and paragons of empathy on the other. I don't think I realised for quite some time how similar we'd made Matthew and Helen to how Pearl reported Angus and Marjorie as being. And all our invented scenarios for couples we saw in restaurants, theatres, and concerts were the same. This doubtless said more about us than anything. All I was really aware of at the time was that I had grown to hate it. And Pearl.

In the end I couldn't take it any longer, so when I was interviewed for and then offered a position in the administration department of Birmingham Children's Hospital I almost fell over myself to accept it: even though traveling to Birmingham instead of Westfield would take longer and cost more, and even though the starting salary was actually less than I was now making in the Security Department at Westfield. My mother was not happy about that, but was sufficiently mollified when I pointed out the multiple opportunities for advancement in such a huge organisation. From my point of view there would also be, I hoped, plenty of available men – young and handsome doctors, with Angus-like personalities – right at hand.

Pearl was suitably gobsmacked when I gave her my news and – typical bloody Pearl, I thought nastily – shocked me in return by telling me that she and her mother had just bought a house in Bournemouth and would be moving there within three months. So no nasty asthma attack ensued.

'I was afraid to tell you, Alice dear, I was afraid you'd be so sad that I was leaving. And now you're leaving... which is such a shame. You would have had my job; it was all arranged with Officer Stevens. Now he'll have to find a new secretary *and* a new junior. He's not going to like that. He was counting on you.'

My inner conflict lasted a very short time. Yes, it would have meant a pay rise and a jump in status. Somebody else would have to make the tea and fetch the damned round sliced milk loaf, but spending the rest of my life working in this stagnant pond? No, no, a thousand times NO! Even without Pearl, it was not what I wanted for even the briefest possible time. Besides, it crossed my mind that this planned move to Bournemouth might be another of Pearl's fantasies anyway; as might the 'arrangement' with Officer Stevens for my putative promotion. And in any case, how dare she set all this up and not tell me? I was supposed to be her best friend, even if she wasn't mine.

My last day at the Security Department office was weird. After a lot of coaching and nagging from Pat I'd promised her that I would not leave without confronting Pearl about her inventions, but I was dreading it. I didn't know how to bring it up or how to react to whatever her response was. And I had no idea at all of what that response might be. There'd been no sign of her asthma returning at the news that I was leaving, but the sort of confrontation this could turn out to be might very well be a different story. Reminding myself I wouldn't be there to pick up the pieces anyway, I rehearsed the speech in my head all morning, but said nothing when Pearl left for lunch, and nothing when she returned. It wasn't until I was about to make our last cups of tea at three o'clock that I finally found a way to start the conversation. I took a deep breath and plunged in.

'Pearl, I have to ask you this.' She turned to look at me expectantly, one earring adrift and perilously close to falling off as usual. Another deep breath and, 'Why did you phone me all those lunchtimes, pretending to be Marjorie?' When it came right down to it, it wasn't so hard to put into words. I stood at the door to our glass corridor, ready to leave to make the tea, and waited.

Pearl snapped her head sharply from side to side looking, I thought bizarrely, more like a peacock than a person, then said 'What on earth are you talking about, Alice?'

'You *know* what I'm talking about, Pearl. You phoned here on countless lunchtimes, from a phone box, pretending to be Marjorie asking about you.'

She stared at me for a few seconds, then shook her head sorrowfully and said, 'Alice, I think you must be mad.'

Something snapped for me. '*Mad*? I'm mad? I rather think not, Pearl, I rather think the boot is on the other foot. It was mad to tell me that Marjorie had heard Helen and Matthew speak right out of *Pilgrim Cottage* as well. Did you think I wouldn't notice you'd used exactly the same expression? *That's* what mad is, Pearl.'

'Oh Alice, Alice... what's happened to you?' Her eyes looked frighteningly wild to me. Never mind an asthma attack – a stroke seemed more likely at this point. 'I don't even know what you're talking about.'

The Pilgrim Cottage Omnibus had long since been returned to the library or I would have insisted on showing her the words on the page. Instead I gave up and left to make the tea, slamming the door behind me just enough to rattle the glass (and Pearl) but not enough to alarm the officers upstairs.

I took my time, struggling to manage my anger and adrenalin rush, putting the three cups for the men on a tray to take upstairs. As I delivered them, one at a time to their various offices, they all said more or less the same thing in response to my 'Last cup of tea from me, Officer whatever.' As if this was the recognised standard response to such a statement, each one said his own version of, 'Well, I hope you haven't put any arsenic in it.'

I responded with a dutiful but insincere smile, said goodbye and thank you, and went back down to the kitchen where I picked up the tea cups for Pearl and me. Not unexpectedly she was drooping over her typewriter and I could actually feel the heaviness of emotion in the air. She looked up miserably as I put the cup down on her desk.

'Oh Alice… Oh my dear, dear, Alice… what can I say?'

I shrugged. I couldn't tell where she was going with this, but at least there was no sign of an asthma attack or a stroke yet. That was something to be thankful for.

'I really didn't want to tell you this, but I should have known you'd rumble me – you're so much cleverer than me, sweet clever Alice. No, I did it for you, Alice, I did it so you wouldn't be hurt.'

'*Hurt*? What do you mean, "hurt"?' I knew I hadn't been able to predict Pearl's response, but this seemed even weirder than anything I could possibly have imagined.

'I only did it after Marjorie stopped ringing you and you were so hurt and I couldn't bear that for you. You are so important to me that when you are sad, I feel an unbearable sadness. I feel it *here,'* pressing her scraggy hand to her saggy bosom and causing me to wonder if I would be sick right here in the office – and if that ghastly cheap-looking marquisate ring had ever really fit her skinny finger.

In some ways this was the biggest reality challenge of all. When had I been hurt? Had we had a conversation about this? Had I been present? I had not actually been aware that Marjorie had stopped ringing – she *hadn't*, until she lost the baby, and *nobody* had rung since then. But somehow, whilst I was making the tea, Pearl had crafted a scenario to make herself look okay about phoning me countless times and pretending to be somebody else… and I was now supposed to be grateful. She constantly praised my supposed cleverness, but hers, here, was beyond belief, beyond anything I might have contrived. Paralleling her bemusement at my challenge, I was now shaking my head in total non-comprehension of what was happening or had happened.

'Don't let it come between us, dearest Alice. It was perhaps wrong of me, but try to remember I was only doing it to save your feelings.'

I sat at my desk with my back to Pearl, closed my eyes and drank my tea. I could actually *see* her, in my mind's eye, climbing inexorably up to the moral high ground. I thought of my promise to Pat about confronting Pearl on all her inventions, but I'd lost heart. In my head I was saying 'and what about Cyril? And friend Matthew? And the Brownes (with an e)? Did you invent them all to stop me being hurt?' And the Henry drama: what about that?' But I said none of it. Perhaps I'd made my point, but I doubted it. I was defeated. And, in a way, she was right. I *was* mad; no sane person would have played The Game with anything like the gusto I had, they wouldn't have played it at all. They wouldn't even have thought about playing it. Sane people didn't need to pretend to be somebody else.

I finished my tea and collected the cups from upstairs to wash them up. I decided I'd leave immediately; they could hardly fire me, after all. I didn't even say goodbye to Pearl: I was actually just about to when the phone rang and, fittingly, it was Edna Betty. I put her through to Officer Stevens, waited for him to ring down and ask for Pearl, connected her to him and him to her, and left whilst she was listening to him ask her to ask me to fetch him a round sliced milk loaf from Wimbushes. Pearl could put whatever spin she liked on it, but once I closed the front door silently behind me and strode – practically ran – towards to the bus station I was free. I never wanted to see her, them, or that part of Westfield for as long as I lived.

TWENTY

It was nearly fifteen years before I saw Pearl again. She and Mother did indeed move to Bournemouth and she sent me her new address, together with a long typed letter about how wonderful her new life was, how she'd made so many 'lovely, lovely' friends – all of whom cared and worried about her *so much,* because her health had deteriorated badly. She'd found a job as secretary in the Farmers' Union, and *nobody, ever!* in that office had had as many birthday cards as she'd had that year. She didn't mention the Brownes, or Angus and Marjorie, and of course she didn't mention The Game. I hadn't replied. I couldn't think of anything I had to say and it wouldn't have been kind to comment on her continuing misplacement of the apostrophe in the words don't and can't.

I hadn't liked my new job. None of the lovely doctors I'd hoped for had materialised. I'd actually had to *work* and it was mind-numbing, soul-destroying filing and typing orders for hospital administration supplies for the most part, day in, day out. So in another of my sudden impulse moves (number four, I think) I'd left after ten months and gone to America on a year's contract as a nanny. I hadn't liked that either, so (impulse number five) had broken my contract and got another dreary job to earn enough money to buy a ticket back home. Back home to what, I hadn't stopped to think. I just knew I had to get there and start my life all over again. I'd done it before, so presumably I could do it again.

But my personal wheel of fortune had suddenly turned itself the right way up and I'd met the man of my dreams, Giles. Miraculously he was even *better* than Pearl's creation of Angus, and how she and I had made Matthew Dexter, and not only because he was actually real flesh and blood rather than a fantasy. I was in love and well loved, and together we had three children. Then, after the third, I hadn't been able to resist contacting old Romantic Pearl to gloat. She, of course, responded immediately with nothing short of her habitual fulsome phrases about how I deserved *such* happiness and if we *ever* came to England on holiday we *must* come and stay with her. The house was her own now, Mother had died and she was *free,* and having *such* a lovely time. Just reading her letter with its over-use of italics (and misplaced apostrophes) made me tired.

I had, of course, told Giles about Pearl, but not about The Game. I didn't think he'd be able to understand that, mostly because it was not a sexual thing. I felt that men probably saw everything as sexual and so he would have no way to comprehend what The Game was all about. I didn't understand it myself anyway, and felt a deep shame at my part in it, all the more so because I now no longer needed to fantasise about people I didn't know – or Bruce – and could hardly remember what it felt like to have that urge. I was now living a real life. Giles was a psychologist, involved more in researching statistics and probabilities than clinical issues, but satisfyingly interested in my Pearl stories, and trained enough to give her behaviour a name – erotomania – thus adding a professionalism to my mother's view of middle-aged spinsters who are thwarted in the love stakes going bonkers. I tried not to think of how close I might have come to falling victim to the same disorder. Actually, Giles was probably better placed to understand our fantasy game than I was, but I never felt I could take the chance. I didn't want a diagnostic label and I definitely didn't want to risk losing his love and respect.

We actually accepted her invitation. Well, we visited her on our annual holiday in the UK, but wisely stayed in a hotel ('easier, with the children...' I told her). But not before she sent another of her novella-length letters about the *lovely* locum doctor who'd come to the house to treat her *life-threatening* asthma attack last year and, guess what, had fallen in love with her – well into her fifties. She didn't say how old he was, but wrote at length about how much she loved him, too. She had also, she confided, been diagnosed with a terminal brain tumour but was at peace with this, thanks to her deep belief in a God who would send her nothing too hard to bear.

Sadly, the doctor – whose name, amazingly enough, was Matthew! – wasn't free to marry her, though of course he desperately wanted to. He already had a wife, a mad wife no less (hello, Mr and Mrs Rochester) back in South Africa where he was from, and where he'd significantly helped Dr Christian

Barnard with the first ever heart transplant but had been too modest to get any publicity. (Crikey! Talk about grandiosity...) Matthew had been tricked into marrying this woman because she'd told him she was pregnant with his baby, but then mysteriously had fallen downstairs and lost the baby. Now she couldn't have children and had 'gone mad'. Giles and I looked forward to her letters with a ghoulish anticipation and he, bless him, said he could hardly wait to meet her.

Leaving the children with my mother (I couldn't inflict her on my poor innocents, no matter how badly I wanted to show them off) we drove down to Bournemouth to spend a reality-challenging afternoon in her bungalow. Giles behaved himself, but only just; somehow managing to stop himself commenting on the dark blue circles under and around her eyes that looked suspiciously like eye shadow to me. I could tell that his sympathetic questioning was designed to give us lots to laugh about later, and oddly, I found I didn't like that. Pearl was certainly maddeningly elusive with facts, but I think my mother was probably right about women of a certain age – some of them, anyway – going a bit nutty when their love life didn't work out too well. And I suddenly felt more sorry for Pearl than anything else.

We had hoped to meet Dr Matthew who was, Pearl had told me, staying with her for the entire summer. (Did he not have a job?) But he was out (I could hear Pat in my head saying 'of *course* he was bloody out!') and would not be back until late that evening, 'after you've left' she said firmly. Giles made her promise that next year we would all go out for a meal, so please make sure he isn't 'out' then. That sealed his fate of course, and four months before our planned visit the following year we heard from Pearl that Matthew had had a 'massive' heart attack and died in her arms. 'Now you're a double murderer', Pat said.

Pearl showed us his photograph in a garishly ornate silver frame on top of her television, but it seemed quite blurred and indistinct to me. Giles, bless him, told me later he'd taken it out of the frame for a closer look when Pearl had shepherded me into her bedroom to show me her prayer desk – on top of which was an open and much-used pot of dusky blue eye shadow – and discovered it was a photocopy of a newspaper photograph of the Bishop of Basingstoke. I don't know why, but that little detail stopped me in my tracks. The last remnants of my sneering anger disappeared and I felt terribly sad for this strange little soul who needed to live in such a fantasy world. A world I might easily have inhabited with her or alongside her, but had somehow managed to escape.

Seven years later I had a phone call – to our home in the United States – from a woman with a distinctly Midlands accent, who announced herself as Pauline Stewart. I couldn't place her until she said 'You may know me as Polly Carter – Stewart is my married name, and Polly is what our mutual friend Pearl called me. Nobody calls me that now though. That was special for Pearl and I shan't be using it again.'

She had rung to tell me that Pearl had died. Not from her brain tumour; that had been 'miraculously cured' through prayer by the nuns at Walsingham, but from heart failure and pneumonia following a devastating series of asthma attacks.

'I've been sorting through her things because I know she'd have wanted you to have something to remember her by.'

'Oh... yes... thank you, that's very kind.'

'After a lot of thought, I've decided to send you her marquisate ring; I know she wore it all the time in her Westfield days, so I think that's the best thing for you to have.'

I was speechless. That ring, swivelling round on Pearl's bony finger, had frankly absolutely repulsed me, but I thanked her as graciously as I could, knowing I wouldn't even open the package when it arrived; it would go straight to the local thrift shop (as they call charity shops in America).

'She was a very special person,' said Polly/Pauline, 'There'll never be anyone like her again in my life.'

'Nor mine,' I agreed, knowing Giles would appreciate the irony even if Polly didn't.

'But it was time,' she continued. 'I'm sorry to say this, but I'm afraid she was going a little strange in the head, you know.'

For the first time in my quarter of a century on-and-off connection with Miss Brenda Pearl Taylor, the only thing I felt for her was profound compassion. When I hung up the phone I really wanted to cry for her and for the life she'd never had, but somehow the tears wouldn't come. I was numb.

* * *

About the Author

Margaret Pitz has spent a lifetime telling herself stories, some of which she has written down and published as novels. Her training and experience as a psychotherapist have helped her understanding of some of the darker motivations of characters in her books. **Alice in Madland** is her third published novel.

Also by the Author

Finding Dad (2013)

10-year-old Jessie Pike sets off to find her father, leaving an uncaring mother and abusive stepfather. She is picked up by Will, a man who will stop at nothing to fulfil a specific fantasy. Will's dream requires Jessie to become someone else, but to what extent is it possible to brainwash a child? And could Jessie's search for father coincide with Will's fantasy? This novel raises fundamental questions about the adult-child relationship that will linger in your mind long after you've read the final page.

Praise for *Finding Dad*:

"Full of insight, humanity and suspense, it offers much food for thought . . . an unusual, uneasy, even shocking read, skilfully told by an author who enters the minds of her characters and brings them to life on the pages." (Reviews: Amazon.co.uk)

After Dad (2014)

A coming-of-age story with a difference, **After Dad** is the story of Ariel (formerly Jessie Pike) and her emergence into the world after spending two years as the often-willing abductee of Will, a man whose fantasy required the two of them to become two other people entirely. This is the story of her emotional healing and re-entry into normal life as she absorbs and comes to terms with the horror of what happened to her in those two missing years.

Praise for *After Dad*:

"Powerful, but gently appointed, a book for someone looking for a really good read...." (Reviews: Amazon.co.uk)